Dreamers

T.J. Baer

Winnipeg, Canada

Developmental editor: Craig Gibb
Proofreader: Alison Cybe

Published May 2024 by Deep Hearts YA, an imprint of Story Perfect Inc.

Deep Hearts YA
PO Box 51053 Tyndall Park
Winnipeg, Manitoba R2X 3B0
Canada

Visit deepheartsya.com for more great reads.

Dreamers

Chapter One

My dad taught me how to dream.

I'd always thought it was pretty simple—you know, fall asleep, dream about flying or falling or illogically losing your pants, wake up some time later with your mouth feeling weird and gummy—but one night he crept into my dreams like a burglar and showed me how it was done.

"The first step," Dad said, towering over me in the dreamscape like he always had in real life, "is realizing you're in a dream. Without that realization, the dream controls you instead of you controlling the dream."

He waved his hand at our surroundings, and I looked around with a cold knot of shame in my chest. The dream had frozen when my dad appeared, leaving my classmates locked in place at their desks, all of them turned to stare at me with disgust or laughter twisting their features. Mr. Raines' kind face was lined with disappointment, and my four younger sisters peered through the classroom window from the bushes outside, fingers clutching the sill and mouths wide with shock and revulsion.

Dad glanced from the hate-filled faces to me, and his expression softened. He was about to say something that would just fill me with more shame, so I shoved down my angsty feelings and asked, "What's step two?"

Dad's thick eyebrows furrowed, but he continued without comment. "The second step is to find the intention to change what you see. It's about willpower, ___."

I flinched but didn't correct him. He had no way of knowing, and it seemed unfair to force a man who had died three years earlier to call me by a name he'd never known.

"You focus on what you want to happen, and then you make it happen. You believe it will, and then it does."

He rested his hand on my shoulder, and I noticed he was looking a little faded around the edges, as if my dream was catching up with the fact that he was dead from a heart attack at age fifty-four and shouldn't actually be here at all.

The old, tucked away grief bit at my throat again. "Dad, is this real? Are you really here?"

Dad smiled. He had light brown eyes like mine, and a manly growth of stubble on his square jaw I would've killed to be able to imitate. He was wearing the shirt I always pictured him in, a faded gray Steelers sweatshirt, along with his most worn-out pair of blue jeans with rips in the knees. I usually dreamed about sitting in the passenger seat of his rattly old pickup truck, breathing in a potent cocktail of leather and exhaust and aftershave, and in those dreams he drove us along sun-dappled roads and sang along to "American Pie" and sometimes glanced over at me with a proud, sad smile.

This was different, though. This wasn't a bleached out memory. I could feel the realness of his presence, the solidity of his hand on my shoulder.

I blinked back the sudden sting of tears from my eyes. "I miss you," I said. "Will I see you again?"

He vanished before he could answer, and I woke up.

Morning in our house was usually a cheerful sort of chaos, but the Monday before my sixteenth birthday was oddly calm. The only hint of mayhem was nine-year-old Eleanor flying down the stairs with ribbons streaming from her double ponytails, shouting about Maribel having stolen her shirt or her lunch or her pencil case or something. It was hard to tell, because her voice kept getting higher and higher until I wasn't sure there were even words in it anymore. Mom popped a lid over the pancakes to keep them warm and flashed me a wry smile as she went upstairs to take care of it.

Mom was like a purposeful, organized hurricane. She swept through our house putting out fires and mediating fights and tucking shoes into closets and books onto shelves. There was no question in anyone's mind that the house would've crumbled or burned down long ago if she weren't there keeping it upright and intact. She was an architect and a single parent and she approached both jobs with the same tidy, logical mind, but she was also warm and smart and funny and sometimes sat on the porch swing with her arms around her legs, staring out at the half-built treehouse Dad had never managed to finish.

While Mom was upstairs separating Eleanor's property from Maribel's person, Jasmine jogged down the stairs and took the last few steps at a jump, hitting the kitchen floor at the base of the stairs like a gymnast, arms held high as if waiting for applause and adoration.

"Hey." I shoveled another spoonful of cereal into my mouth. "Your shirt's on backwards again."

At fourteen, Jasmine was the oldest of my sisters. We'd been like twins for a long time despite our age difference, sharing clothes, wearing our hair the same way, and speaking in sentence fragments only we understood. In the last year or so, Jasmine had gone the route of dyed blond hair, elaborate makeup, and tight, fashionable clothes, while I'd gone…well, a different direction.

Jasmine smirked as she grabbed the cereal box from in front of me. "Peasant," she said with a dignified lift of her chin. "I told you, this is the style. What are *you* wearing?"

Truthfully, I'd been waiting for Mom to make a comment about my outfit all morning, but while I'd felt her eyes on my back as I made breakfast, she'd never actually said anything about it. I tugged at my oversized gray sweatshirt and folded my jean-clad legs at the ankle, my feet in their ratty red sneakers seeking refuge under my chair.

"It's comfortable." I slouched my shoulders in a way I'd been practicing in the mirror and was pleased to see a flat expanse of fabric camouflaging my chest. "The first day of school's bad enough without having to squeeze myself into some awful, tight-fitting—"

Jasmine arched an eyebrow and waved a manicured hand at her own snug blue top and skirt.

"Ahem." I ducked my head to hide a smile. "What I mean to say is, this is what makes me feel comfortable, so I'm wearing it."

"All right," Jasmine said with a roll of her eyes. "Whatever you say, ___."

I edited out the word right after she said it, and I told myself that very soon I'd be brave enough to tell my family. I'd tell them and they'd understand and it would all be okay. Sure.

Jasmine's back was to me as she poured almond milk over her cereal, and I thought we were done talking, so I went back to frowning at the word jumble in the newspaper. But before I'd untangled SIEUIDGS, Jasmine cleared her throat.

"Hey, so I heard Jackson call you 'Leo' the other day. What's that about?"

I froze, then realized I needed to play things cool but not quite *that* cool and forced a smile. "Oh, it's just a nickname. I can't even remember how it started. You know Jackson."

"Huh." Jasmine's gaze stayed locked on my face for a second too long before she shrugged and slid the cereal box into its Mom-ordained place in our impeccably organized cupboard. "I guess it just made me think about that one summer when we were little and you started asking everybody to call you 'Sam.' That was weird, right? Mom was so glad when you grew out of it. She was afraid she was going to have to ask the teachers at school to change your name on the attendance sheet or something."

I flinched. Was the idea of me choosing a name for myself really so ridiculous? Mom had humored me at the time, calling me by the name I'd asked to be called, but apparently the whole time she'd been quietly wishing I would stop.

I was still trying to figure out what to say—or if I needed to say anything—when Mom swept back into the kitchen with her usual steady smile.

"Have twins, they said. It'll be fun, they said." She laughed and brushed her dark curls out of her eyes. "Well, at least that's all sorted out for now with a minimum of hair-pulling and tantrums." She ducked in to plant a good morning kiss on Jasmine's cheek, then rubbed off the resulting smear of lipstick with her thumb. "You look nice. I know the first day of school doesn't seem like such a big deal, but it really is a great time to make a good impression."

Jasmine shot me a significant look I did my best to ignore. "Thanks, Mom. That's what I'm aiming for. Making an impression."

"She said a *good* impression," I muttered into my teacup, and Jasmine shot me a dirty look over one shoulder.

"Anyway." Jasmine turned appealing, long-lashed dark eyes on our mother. "Do you think you could give me a lift to school this morning? I wouldn't ask, but I do want to make a good impression, and I'm just picturing these white shoes on that grimy bus floor…"

Mom gave a pained smile. "Honey, I'd love to, but you know I have that big meeting this morning."

Jasmine sighed. "I guess I can always bleach them when I get home."

Mom shot me a pleading look, and I breathed a sigh of my own as I turned to Jasmine.

"Look, do you want to ride with Jackson and me?

There's room in the backseat, and except for a few gum wrappers, it's probably way cleaner than the bus."

Jasmine looked from Mom's innocent face to my pinched one and apparently decided the value of the favor was worth ignoring how it had come about. "Yes, thank you! That'd be awesome! I'll go get my stuff. Don't leave without me!"

She inhaled one last bite of cereal and dashed upstairs in a wash of blond hair and flowery scent, and I sighed again and slouched deeper in my chair. Mom squeezed my shoulder and gave me one of her patented *I'm proud of you* smiles.

"Thank you for doing that. I know it's got to be weird having your sister along when you're trying to spend quality time with your boyfriend, but it means a lot to her."

I was warmed by the thanks and then bristled at the word "boyfriend."

"Mom, I told you, Jackson and I are just friends."

"Sure, sure." Mom's smile was secretive and knowing as she left a red lipstick print on her A WOMAN'S PLACE IS IN THE REVOLUTION coffee cup. "Whatever you say. Speaking of, will your special friend be coming to your birthday party?"

Special friend. I rolled my eyes. "No, because you said it was going to be a family gathering and a 'formal occasion,' and I figured that both of those things excluded Jackson."

"Probably true," Mom said. "But if you wanted to invite him…I mean, if there was any particular reason why you would want him to be there to celebrate this very special day with you…"

"*Mom.*"

"Fine, fine. Just keep it in mind."

I held back the words for an impressive count of five and then exploded, "Anyway, I don't see why we have to have a big fancy party just because it's my birthday. We never have before."

"You've never turned sixteen before," Mom said calmly. Calm was her best weapon against emotional children and emotional clients, and she'd been using it effectively against both for years. "It's an important milestone, and our family wants to be there for it. And if they're going to go to all the trouble of flying here from halfway across the country, the least we can do is give them a nice party."

"I thought the party was supposed to be for me."

She looked at me like I'd completely missed the point, then squinted at my face and leaned closer.

I ducked back self-consciously. "What?"

"We'll have to schedule you for a lip wax before the party," she said. "I'd say we should blame your father's genes for that, but I think we both know that's a lie." She glanced at her watch and tucked her coffee mug into the top rack of the dishwasher. "I'd better get going. Tell the twins to eat their pancakes before they get cold, tell Eliza her summer reading list is on the counter, and don't forget to lock the door when you leave. And make sure you and Jasmine wear your seatbelts!"

"We will," I said tiredly as the hurricane grabbed her briefcase from the counter and swept out into the hall and toward the front door.

"Bye, girls!" Mom shouted. "I love you! Have a great day at school!"

There was a chorus of muffled replies from upstairs, but the goodbyes and love yous stuck in my throat, not because I didn't want to say them, but because Mom's words had been directed at "girls" and I wasn't one.

In the end, I gave a strangled, "Bye, love you!" and listened to the door slam shut and my mother's heels pound a quick rhythm across the porch. Her car started in the driveway, and I sank my head into my arms until all I could smell was the clean, comforting scent of my freshly-laundered sweatshirt and the men's deodorant I'd put on that morning. I thought about the blue-sequined dress hanging in my closet, pushed to the very back but lying in wait for me like a predator, and a rush of determination momentarily drowned out the utter certainty that I was about to ruin my life.

"All right, Leo," I mumbled into my arms. "You can do this. You can absolutely do this."

I wasn't so sure that I could, but I also couldn't spend my whole life hiding in the arms of my sweatshirt. I got up, rinsed out my bowl, and got ready for the day that was going to change everything.

Chapter Two

"Hey, thanks for doing this," I said as I yanked open the passenger door of Jackson's battered Toyota.

Jackson looked cool as always with his gelled black hair and crooked smile. His features were small and elfin, his nose and chin pointed like an old-school illustration of Peter Pan. Freckles chased across his cheeks and past the silver stud in his nose. "No problem, my man," he said. I hated that I had to glance over my shoulder to make sure Jasmine wasn't close enough to hear me being called "my man." "We're heading to school with an empty backseat or a full one, so no skin off my nose either way, you know?"

Jasmine was there a few seconds later, a bright blue plastic backpack slung over one shoulder and a knitted sweater draped over her arm. "Hey, Jackson, thanks so much for the ride!"

"Like I was just telling—" He caught my warning glance and shifted gears smoothly. "Like I was just saying, we're going to school either way, so it doesn't make much difference if you're here or not."

Jasmine frowned a little like she wasn't sure if this was an insult or not—it wasn't, but I didn't bother to share that information—then shrugged and slid into the backseat. She had to move a few books, a sweatshirt, and a box of cereal out of the way to do it, but she did so without complaint and settled happily into a seat that was not attached to a rowdy, filthy bus of our peers.

"Mom said to make sure to buckle up," I said, mostly joking, because we'd been told to buckle up for so long that the idea of not buckling up would never have occurred to either of us. "And you might want to have your earbuds ready. Jackson's taste in music is not for everyone."

Jackson tossed me a lazy frown as he pushed his sunglasses up over his gelled hair. "I thought you liked Korean death metal."

"I mean, *I* do," I said. "Of course, I do. It's just not everybody's cup of tea. Some people prefer songs where your brains don't bleed out of your ears while you're listening to them, for instance."

Jackson gave an offended scoff and got us underway with a rumble from the engine and an expert twist of the steering wheel. "Well, since you texted and said Jas would be joining us, I actually made a special playlist just for the occasion."

Jasmine perked up in the back seat. For all that she'd never really understood why I liked hanging out with Jackson, he was a reasonably attractive individual who fell under the broad category of "guy," and thus any special favor from him was bound to pique her interest. "You did? For me?"

"That's right." Jackson pressed a button on his phone and the first few chords of what sounded like "My Heart

Will Go On" being massacred by a chorus of electric guitars blared through the speakers. "You like love songs, right?" he shouted as the lead singer began to scream something in Korean that sounded fractionally less angry than Jackson's usual musical selections. "This is all love songs!"

"Great!" Jasmine yelled back. She pointedly pulled out her earbuds and plugged them into her ears.

Jackson waited ten or so seconds, then turned the volume down to the point where we could hear the tinny beat of a pop song from Jasmine's neon yellow earbuds. My ears were still ringing with the echoes of screamed Korean love, but it faded mercifully quickly.

"I wanted to tell you." Jackson's voice was pitched so low Jasmine probably wouldn't have heard him over the noise of the engine even if her eardrums weren't being blasted by cheery girl pop. "I got something in the mail yesterday."

My heart stammered in my chest. "Oh, yeah?"

"I didn't open it—I figured that's personal stuff and you should open it on your own—but I've got it in the trunk. Don't let me forget to give it to you later."

Jasmine's head was still bopping in the rearview mirror, her gaze sliding over the landscape passing by the window.

"Do you think you could give it to me right after we get to school? I'd kind of like to wear it today."

Jackson arched a dark eyebrow at me. The silver piercing in it glittered in the sunlight shining through the windshield, and I remembered his mother nearly passing out when he'd first come home with his piercings. She'd cried something in Korean and flopped back onto the sofa like a dead fish, and it had been both worrying and oddly hilarious.

"You're supposed to wear those things in before you have 'em on for a long time, you know," he said. "You gotta stretch 'em out."

"I know." And I did, but I was too excited, and too determined that this year was going to be a fresh start, a new me. The real me. "Look, I know it sounds nuts, but I just—I want to feel like myself, you know? And if this can help me do it…"

"I get it." There was a soft note to his voice that made me remember a younger Jackson showing up at my back door in tears, confessing over Monty Python and a pint of ice cream that he was pretty sure he was gay and in love with the goth boy next door, and neither of those things were likely to end well when you were the son of a deeply Republican minister and a melodramatic hairdresser. "I just want you to be careful. If it starts hurting, or you start feeling dizzy or lightheaded or something—"

"I'll take it off immediately."

He shot me one last cautious look before returning his eyes to the road. "And hey, I've been looking through some of Mom's magazines, and I think there's something we can do to your hair to make it look more, you know. Manly. Give me five minutes and I'll work my magic, 'kay?"

Manly hair, manly clothes, flat chest. This was really happening. Butterflies erupted in my stomach at the hugeness of what I was doing, but I'd come too far to back out now.

"I have to see Ms. Hernández before class," I said, "but

I'm pretty sure I can spare five minutes for a makeover montage."

Jackson's sunglasses had slid back over his eyes, but I could still sense the concern as he glanced over at me. "You sure you're up for this, man?"

I released a breath in a shaky exhale. "It's gotta happen sometime. And it might as well be now."

I'd been worried Jasmine might hang around after we got to school, but she was out the door with a shouted "Thanks again!" before Jackson even set the parking brake. I waited until she'd joined the crowd of students milling around the front entrance of the school before I turned to Jackson and tried not to bounce in my seat from excitement.

Jackson rolled his eyes at me, a grin tugging at his lips. "All right, settle down. I'll get it."

I climbed out of the car and watched as he jiggled the key in the Toyota's trunk, gave the back of the car a few expert raps with his fist and foot, and glared at the trunk until it popped open. A package waited inside, not a box but a slim plasticky parcel that moved like cloth when it was lifted. Jackson lowered it into my waiting hands with all the gravitas of a sacred ceremony.

"Your binder, good sir."

My breath caught, the package seeming to tingle beneath my fingers. I imagined what I would look like with the binder on, how it would change everything. Or if not everything, at least enough. *Please let it be enough.*

"All right," Jackson said with a laugh, "I can see you're

gonna explode if you don't go put it on, so get going. Meet you at your favorite bathroom in five."

I gave him a brotherly slap on the shoulder, then hugged the package to my chest and ran for the school. My "favorite bathroom," as Jackson had dubbed it, was the only unisex toilet in the building. It was a single, too, which suited me just fine, and it had a traditional sit-down commode as well as a urinal, perfect for practicing before I made the eventual leap to using the men's room. But hey, one step at a time.

I crashed into the bathroom like my own mini version of Mom's hurricane and locked the door. The package was open and the wrapping in tatters in the trashcan before the echoes of the lock clicking had even faded from the room.

And there it was, in my hands. My first binder.

It was a white half-tank that had come highly recommended by the online trans groups I belonged to, and while it looked ludicrously small to squeeze onto my body, I knew it would fit. This was the day I started along a new, better path, and the fact that the binder had happened to come just in time had to mean I was meant to wear it, and it was meant to fit.

Several minutes later, when I heard a knock on the door and Jackson's quiet, "Leo? You okay in there, buddy?" I had to admit I had perhaps been mistaken.

"Um," I said in a strangled voice, "kind of?"

There was a pause, as if Jackson was looking both ways down the hall to make sure no one was around. "What do you mean? Is it on?"

"Not exactly. It's kind of…stuck."

"Stuck?"

I gave myself a weary glance in the mirror. The lower band of the binder was cutting into my small but irritatingly existent chest, stuck right in the middle of what I'd started to refer to as my "man boobs." While one of the straps was digging into my right bicep, trapping my arm to my side, the other was under my left armpit and seemed like it might need scissors or some kind of heavy-duty chainsaw to remove.

Jackson sighed. "All right, open the door."

Alarm tore through me. "I *can't*. I'm not—All I'm wearing is pants and this binder, and it's not covering stuff, if you know what I mean."

"Look, man, if you're really stuck, then you're gonna have to either let me in or get real comfy in that bathroom, because you might just have to live there now. Unless you want me to call the fire department?"

I let out a wordless cry of frustration and managed to maneuver my body so the arm trapped at my side could flick the lock open. "Don't laugh."

Jackson slipped inside and locked the door behind him. There was a cautious look in his eyes and a firm non-smile on his face, but his lips twitched when he caught sight of the predicament I was in.

"Well," he said.

"You promised not to laugh."

"I didn't, actually, and I'm *not*." He studied me for a moment, then took a deep breath. "Is it okay if I…you know, help?"

"Please," I said miserably.

He managed to dig his fingers under this strap and then that strap and somehow got them settled into place on my shoulders, and then it was just a matter of tugging the bottom of the binder down a few inches so it settled where it was supposed to. My arms and shoulders ached and my skin was slashed pink from where the fabric had cut into it, but the binder was on. Thank God and thank Jackson, it was on.

"Better?" Jackson asked as he stepped back to survey his work.

"Much." I turned around gingerly and faced myself in the mirror.

Now that it was properly on, the binder didn't feel as tight as I'd been fearing—it had been more a case of navigating it over my shoulders and elbows, but it seemed to fit perfectly well now that it was on. It was snug, definitely, but that was the idea, after all. It pressed down on my chest so what was left was flatter, if not perfectly flat, and while it didn't hide the curves that dipped from my rib cage down to my hips, it at least seemed to do the job it had been intended for. Still, I couldn't help a little tug of disappointment at how it hadn't magically transformed my body into a paragon of masculinity, like the act of sliding on this tight half-tank should have morphed my body into exactly what I wanted it to be.

"It'll probably look better with a shirt over it," Jackson suggested gently, and I dug my gray T-shirt and blue plaid flannel out of my half-open backpack. I'd been wearing them under my baggy sweatshirt before, but after I slipped them on, I left the sweatshirt where it lay by the bathroom sink and faced my reflection.

A tentative smile pulled at my lips as I gazed at myself. It wasn't perfect, but it was pretty close. With clothes on top, the effect of the binder was magical. My chest looked flat, and the layered T-shirt/flannel combo made it look all the more so.

"Now." Jackson grinned as he pulled a tin of hair wax out of his bag. "Let's see about that hair."

Chapter Three

I felt eyes on me as I walked down the hallway next to Jackson, but it might've been my imagination. Jackson kept up a stream of idle conversation as we walked, and while I tried to focus on what he was saying, I struggled to manage more than an occasional "hmm" or "uh-uh." I was fully dressed but had the unmistakable dream feeling of striding through school naked, probably because the real me was on display for the first time, and that felt pretty damned terrifying.

But also good. Really, really good.

Jackson dropped me off at Ms. Hernández's office with a brotherly slap to my shoulder and an encouraging, "You got this, man." After he'd gone, I found myself face to face with my reflection in the glass of the closed door.

Jackson had done a miracle job on my hair—sometimes it paid to have a best friend whose mom was a hairstylist—and he'd somehow gelled and styled it so it was less Tinkerbell and more edgy teen guy. I'd had no idea my limp brown locks could be persuaded to sweep forward into a messy series of spiky bangs, but I loved it, and if Jackson couldn't teach me how to do it myself, he was going to be stuck being my personal hairstylist for the rest of his life.

That plus the clothes and the effect of the binder had me moving and feeling more like myself than ever before. My steps swaggered more, my whole body felt looser and more relaxed, and that plus the fuzz I'd been cultivating on my upper lip made me actually look more like the guy I wanted people to see me as. Whether they'd be able to push past years of seeing me as a girl was another matter altogether, but at least now I could look at myself in the mirror and like what I saw. That was definite progress.

I knocked on Ms. Hernández's door and then stepped inside after a casual call from within. I found her sitting behind two large stacks of papers and manila folders, her "VERONICA HERNÁNDEZ, GUIDANCE COUNSELOR" nameplate being used as a paperweight for a messy pile of receipts. Her curly black hair had a pen sticking out of it just over her right ear, and a pair of round red glasses slipped down her nose as she squinted at the piece of paper in her hands. A tremor of nerves shot through me as I waited for her to notice me. This office had been a safe space for me in the past, but would it still be after this?

After what felt like an eternity, Ms. Hernández spared me a glance before returning her gaze to the paper. "Have a seat, young man, and I'll be with you in just a moment."

My heart gave a stumbling jolt of joy at being called a young man, but I'd only gone a few steps toward the chair when the paper was ripped away from Ms. Hernández's face and she gave me a longer look.

"Oh, ___!" she exclaimed. The joy deflated in my chest

like a punctured balloon. "New hair? I didn't recognize you at first. Looks good. Anyway, have a seat and tell me what I can do for you. Don't let all this mess fool you—you have my full attention."

I wasn't sure I did as she rifled through the papers and jotted notes, but I still settled into the chair and took a deep breath.

"I'm here because I want to change the name teachers call me in class."

Ms. Hernández's pen paused mid-jot, and then she pushed her glasses back up onto her nose and laid the pen down. "What do you mean, dear?"

It was too hard to meet her eyes, so I looked down at my fingers. "I mean, I'm not gay, like we thought before. I'm bi or pan if I'm anything, but what I mean to say is, I realized I'm trans. I'm transgender, and the name everybody's been calling me is a girl's name, but I'm not a girl. So I want to use a different name and be referred to as a guy. Because that's what I am."

There was a long silence my nightmares assured me was because Ms. Hernández was aghast, disgusted, horrified. When I finally got the courage to glance at her face, however, I didn't see any of those emotions, just a quiet, appraising look as she studied me.

"Are you sure?" she asked.

"One hundred percent." It felt like releasing a long-held breath as I said it.

Ms. Hernández nodded and gave me a small smile that was only slightly tempered by the worry in her eyes. "All right, then, let's get the process started. What name is it that you want to go by?"

"Leo." The name came from my lips as if I were speaking a holy word that might set a mighty incantation into motion.

This time, her smile seemed more genuine. "All right, Leo. Your old name will still be in all your teachers' gradebooks, but I can give you a note to give to them alerting them to the change. This might take some getting used to, but I'm sure they'll do their best. And if anyone gives you any trouble, you let me or one of your teachers know and we'll sort it out. Do you, uh... Do you want to start using the boys' bathroom?"

A thrill went through me at the realization that this was real, this was happening. "Um, maybe not yet. I've been using the unisex bathroom down by the gym."

Something like relief crossed Ms. Hernández's face. "Okay, that's probably best for now, anyway. Until people get more used to this." She paused with her pen midway through a word. "Does your family know about this? Your mother?"

Heat crept into my cheeks as I shook my head. "But I'm going to tell them. I'm just trying to figure out how to do it."

"Are you sure you want to go forward with this now, then? We can always wait until after you've told them. Word will get around, and I'm sure you'd rather they hear it from you. And, of course, while we can change the name the teachers call you in class, we can't do anything about your name in our systems without paperwork, parental consent, things like that, so…"

I shook my head again. I had to do it this way. This was the only way, because I would never manage to tell my family unless I had no other choice, unless it was a race between me spilling the beans or them finding out from some random person at the supermarket or in line at the bank.

"I'm sure," I said, and Ms. Hernández went back to writing my new school identity into existence.

I wanted to be someone who could walk into class with my head held high, ignoring the whispers around me as I strode to a desk in the front row. Instead, I slouched into a seat in the back by the windows and hoped no one looked at me. Jackson wasn't in my first or second period classes, so it was just me against the world. The only protection I had was the little square of paper clutched in my hand, which I intended to deliver to Mr. Raines the second he walked into class.

There was still a good ten minutes before the bell, though, so Mr. Raines was probably in his usual spot at the big picture window of the library, gazing out across the school lawn with a cup of coffee in his hand and a faint smile on his face. He always waved at Jackson and me as we went by, and sometimes he stood there with a book in his hand and a pair of glasses perched on his nose, while other times he just gazed out into the middle distance with a deeply thoughtful expression as if he were pondering the secrets of the universe.

I switched the paper into my left hand so I could rub my sweaty palm against my jeans. Mr. Raines had been my favorite teacher years before I'd even been in his class, and I had no idea what I would do if he didn't accept this. Accept me. I thought about his soft, patient voice as he made indecipherable math problems make sense, the warm chuckle he gave when a student finally got what he was trying to teach them. He'd never raised his voice or shouted or raged at a student, and somehow he'd never needed to. He was special, and liking him also meant that I wanted him to like me, and this might be the moment he decided he didn't.

As the minutes ticked on, a few heads turned back toward me with frowns and murmurs, but I did my best to ignore them. I didn't know everyone in the class—my grade had picked up fifty or so students from a charter school that had closed down in the spring—but the ones I did know were gazing at me with a mix of curiosity and confusion. I didn't see any signs of hatred yet, but I wasn't so naïve as to think they would never come.

I usually spent the time before class started scribbling story ideas in my notebook or penning terrible sketches of my characters, many of whom were guys who looked and acted suspiciously like me—or, at least, the me I wanted to be—but I was too nervous to vanish into writing mode today. And if today went well, maybe self-insert fiction wouldn't be the only way I could live the life I wanted.

Mr. Raines breezed into the classroom three minutes before the bell, smelling of coffee and old books. His fair hair was less blond and more gray these days, but there was still a youthful smoothness to his face. A pair of plastic-framed brown glasses straight out of the seventies peeked out of the breast pocket of his velvety green suit jacket, and underneath it he wore the typical dress shirt, tie, and slacks combo favored by most of the male teachers at our school, though his slacks had a bit more of a bell-bottom flare. He looked a little tired but otherwise his usual kind self, and he stopped to offer a gentle word or a smile to several students on the way to his desk.

I got to my feet, my hands shaking, and started up the aisle toward him. I was nearly to his desk when he glanced up, glanced back down, and then lifted his eyes again to take a longer look. His gaze traced from my hair to my face to my clothes, and I suddenly couldn't look at him because I didn't want to see how he reacted.

"Ms. Hernández said to give this to you," I mumbled. I handed over the note with my eyes cast downward.

I'd meant to give it to him and then escape back to my seat, but my feet stayed rooted to the spot as he plucked the paper from my hand, unfolded it, and read it. Another silence stretched, one I knew I was going to have to start getting used to.

A warm hand touched my arm and I glanced up in surprise.

"I've always liked the name Leo," Mr. Raines said in his gentlest voice.

He'd used the same voice when he'd found me curled up in a corner of the library crying after Dad died. He'd handed me a box of tissues and then had gone away and come back with two chocolate donuts and a cup of tea liberated from the teachers' lounge. He'd stayed there with me until I felt steady enough to leave, listening to me talk when I needed to but otherwise being kindly and comfortably silent. Just being there. It had been exactly what I needed.

And these words, now, were exactly what I needed, too.

"Me, too," I said, and I returned to my desk feeling one more little drop of courage burning through my veins.

Maybe I could do this after all.

Chapter Four

The moment came at 8:35 AM. Mr. Raines was reading through the roll, pausing to ask for correct pronunciation on the names of some of the new students, and he'd read the A's through S's and was finally to the T's. Mika Takada was marked present, then Kyle Thomas, and then…

"Leo Torres?"

"Here." I tried to pitch my voice low, but it came out weak and cracked, sending a titter of laughter through the class. Mr. Raines caught my eye and gave a small shrug with a smile that said, *Don't worry about it*, then continued through the attendance.

There were definite whispers now from the kids who'd been in my class last year, frowns and backward glances. I tried not to look but couldn't help my gaze flickering here and there in search of hatred or condemnation, my nightmare come to life. It was during one of these flickering glances that I found a face turned toward mine.

The others threw covert looks at me over their shoulders, but this was a face turned directly toward me, a pair of eyes fixed on mine with open interest.

It was a nice face, finely boned and friendly. A mass of

curly reddish-blond hair topped it, large lazy curls spilling over a broad forehead, and then there were eyebrows so fair they were almost invisible, followed by strikingly dark brown eyes. The eyes made me pause, because they should've been blue or green or a light hazel to match the paleness of their surroundings, but instead they were stubbornly, proudly brown despite all expectations. I liked them immediately, and I liked the little half-smile on the full lips below them. I already kind of wanted to write him into a story I was working on.

"Robbie Welsh," Mr. Raines called, and the face turned away from mine to say, "Here."

I watched Robbie Welsh for most of the rest of class, and while he never looked back at me again, his gaze fixed on the notebook in front of him, I felt weirdly like his attention was focused in my direction. It was probably my imagination though, because when the bell rang, he gathered up his things and hurried out of the room without a glance my way.

I got to my feet telling myself I wasn't disappointed. I didn't even know this guy, right? As I stuffed my Geometry book and notebook into my backpack, I was so busy not being disappointed that I didn't realize anyone was approaching me until they were already at my desk, blocking my path to the door.

"Hey." It was Aspen Jacobs, who I'd worked with on a group project once but otherwise hadn't spoken two words to. "Are you ___'s brother or cousin or something?"

Two other girls stood beside her, one I recognized from last year—Carly something—and one who was probably new. Both of them were studying my face in a way that made my palms start sweating.

"Or something," I said, trying again to pitch my voice as low as I could. I'd been watching online tutorials about voice training for weeks, but I still felt like my voice was the one thing that would always give me away.

"Cool," Aspen said. "So if you're looking for someone to sit with at lunch, you can always… I mean, if you want to sit with us…"

"You can totally sit with us." Eagerness was bright in Carly's tone as she leaned toward me. She was twirling one strand of light brown hair around her index finger and it was strangely mesmerizing. "If you want to."

"If you want to," Aspen agreed.

Was this flirting? Were they flirting with me? Good God.

"Um, yeah, thanks," I managed. I made to move for the door, but the girl who hadn't spoken yet—the new girl—held out her hand to stop me. "I'm Maya, by the way. Maya Virani. What was your name again?"

I needed to get out of here. I needed to get away from these girls and their intense stares and maybe-flirting and just *all of it*.

"It's Leo," I said, and then I bolted, ignoring the flutter of laughter that followed me as I all but ran from the room and out into the crowded hallway.

I dodged bodies and open lockers on instinct alone, my breath coming fast as the full weight of what I was doing crashed down on me. Aspen and Carly didn't know me all that well, so it made sense they hadn't really recognized me, and it *was* nice that they'd clearly read me as a boy, but… God. They were going to figure it out. My old classmates were going to know or realize it was me, and they were going to tell the new kids and then everyone was going to know and that was what I'd been expecting but now suddenly I didn't want it.

I wanted a clean start, for people to see me as Leo and not *Leo who used to be* ___ or ___ *who is pretending to be a boy* or whatever awful things they thought. I wanted to show them who I was but I also wanted to hide in the deepest, darkest, safest place I could find, and the sheer heaviness of it all made my binder feel like it was pressing tighter and tighter against my chest. My breath came shallowly and spots formed in front of my eyes, and oh my God, I was going to pass out here in the middle of the hallway. I was going to pass out and they were going to have to cut my binder off of me and—

A cool hand wrapped over my wrist and tugged me over to the water fountain, where I managed to lean down and drink a few lukewarm mouthfuls. The spots still swam in my vision, and my head felt fuzzy enough that I didn't question when I was led down a hallway and into a quiet, empty classroom with the lights off.

"Here, sit down," a voice said. It was pleasantly husky and pitched somewhere between what I'd expect from a guy or girl. I let myself be lowered into a chair and tried to pull myself back from the dizzy brink of passing out. "Do you know 4-7-8 breathing?"

I shook my head.

"In for four, hold for seven, out for eight. Try it. Here."

A hand gripped mine and began to squeeze in a slow rhythm. "Focus on my hand and try the breathing."

I did. The hand was warm and lightly callused, and the rhythmic pulses grounded me, gave me something to concentrate on. I breathed in, held it, released it, then did it again. The bell went but I ignored it, and the fingers wrapped around mine never wavered as the hallway outside filled with the scuffling of feet hurrying to class. I breathed.

Finally, the tightness in my chest began to loosen, and the binder went back to being snug but not suffocating. I took one last slow, even breath and opened my eyes.

It was Robbie Welsh. He'd pulled one of the other desks over to where I sat and was leaning forward, his dark eyes fixed on me. That faint half-smile still touched his lips, but it wasn't laughing at me so much as encouraging me, supporting me.

I tore my gaze away from him, embarrassed. "Sorry."

"Panic attack," he said. It wasn't a question. "I used to get them a lot. Do you want to take off your binder?"

I glanced at him in surprise. "No, it's fine. I was just—It's not the binder, it's me. I mean, maybe it's the binder. It's my first one and I just got it, so—How did you know?"

"I saw the edge of it through your shirt when you were talking to Mr. Raines. I doubt anybody else did, or knew what it was if they saw it. Mine's a zip-up. They say the non-zip kind are better, but I need to be able to zip it down a little if I start feeling suffocated, you know?"

It took my brain a good four or five seconds to catch up. "Wait, you mean. You…?"

"Me."

"Huh. I don't think I've ever met another trans guy before."

He looked amused. "Never?"

"I mean, I've seen a bunch of us online in forums and groups and stuff, but never in person. I thought..."

"What?"

"I thought I was the only one around here. I guess that was dumb, though. I mean, there's a lot of people in this city—in this school, even. Of course there have to be other trans guys around."

Robbie gave a little shrug. "A lot of guys like to go stealth." At my blank stare, he continued, "Not telling people you're trans. Just letting them assume you're a *guy*, not a *trans guy*. It's easier, but sometimes it feels—" He shook his head. "Anyway, it doesn't look like you're going that route, does it?"

He sounded somewhere between wistful and respectful, like I was doing some great heroic thing.

"I don't know what I'm doing," I said. I pressed my face into my hands and let the coolness of my palms seep into my overheated forehead. "I thought that's what I wanted, for everyone to know about me, but I think I just want to be a guy, you know? For people to look at me and know who I am and for it not to be a big thing. I want to be myself and not have to worry about everybody hating me or judging me or—I don't know. I don't want to have to tell people who I am. I just want them to *know*."

Robbie's eyes dropped from mine as a small, sad smile tugged at his lips. "I get it. But hey, looks like you're on the right track. And first binder—big milestone, right? How's it feel? Aside from occasionally suffocating, I mean."

A grin spread across my face. "Fantastic. I mean, I could barely get it on. My friend Jackson had to untangle me, which was pretty freaking embarrassing, but once I got it on… I wish I never had to take it off, or—"

"Or that you didn't need it in the first place," Robbie said, and I nodded.

He got to his feet, and I realized with regret that we really did need to get to second period—and I had to give Mr. Donahue my note from Ms. Hernández. Had he read the roll already? Had everyone in class heard my deadname echoing through the classroom?

Easy, I told myself. *Enough panic for one day. It'll be all right. It'll all be fine.*

Somehow, after meeting Robbie, it was easier to believe that might actually be true.

"What have you got next?" Robbie asked as we pushed our desks back to where they belonged.

"Social Studies. With Mr. Donahue."

He pulled a wrinkled piece of paper from his pocket and squinted at it, then grinned. "Me, too."

I grinned back, and it was strange how natural it felt for him to settle in beside me as we walked. He was a little taller than me, a little wider and more solid, and he wore a layered look similar to my own—dark T-shirt under a collared red button-down, baggy green cargo pants with sneakers. We wore different versions of the same trans boy uniform, and I thought about the zip-up binder he was wearing underneath all this, the body like mine that hid under this nice-looking male exterior.

For the first time in a very long time, I felt less alone.

Chapter Five

"I know this is a dream," I said.

Dad's voice echoed through my dreamscape. "Hey, you got step one. Good job."

When I turned, he was standing behind me in a yellow polo shirt, brown belt, fitted blue jeans, and loafers—the kind of outfit he'd always worn to work. His curly dark hair was still an uncombable mess, but that had always been part of his charm.

"Hey, kiddo," he said.

I smiled and tried not to think about his slack face in the coffin. Last time I'd thought about him being dead he'd started to disappear, and I wanted to hold onto him for longer this time.

"I don't know how long we'll have today," he said.

A lump formed in my throat. "Because you're…"

"Because you're sleeping in study hall," Dad said with a wry arch of his eyebrow.

"Oh." I laughed, and it felt good.

"So, first day seems to be going well, then?" Dad surveyed the dreamscape, which was frozen as it had been last time he'd appeared but this time was a dim, quiet classroom empty except for the smiling figures of Jackson, Mr. Raines, and Robbie Welsh. They sat in a semi-circle facing me, and each of them held a banner that said, "LEO LEO HE'S OUR MAN." It was a little embarrassing, but I couldn't help smiling.

"Leo, huh?" Dad's gaze traced over me, and a glance downward showed that I stood before him as I wanted to be seen, flat chested and for some reason wearing his faded Steelers shirt and ripped jeans. Only the red sneakers were mine. Before I even had a chance to worry about his reaction, he gave a curt nod. "I like it. Suits you. But then I guess it would, since you picked it out."

I wasn't sure what to say, so I just floated in the warm tide of Dad's approval.

"Leo was your abuelo's name, you know."

"I know." I'd never met Dad's parents, as they'd both died in an accident long before I was born, but Dad had told so many stories about Grandpa Leonardo and Grandma Rosa that I felt like I'd always known them. Grandma Rosa had come here from Mexico when she was twelve with two little sisters and no parents, and she'd managed to keep their little family safe and fed and together while they crossed the country to find their aunt and uncle who lived in Pittsburgh. And Grandpa Leo had come from a poor family with ten kids, but he'd grown up to found a big construction company. I still sometimes saw billboards for it on the highway.

"So, hey, let's talk more about dreaming." Dad's voice jarred me from my thoughts. "You've gotten past step one, right? So, it's time to try step two. You think you can handle it?"

"Maybe?"

"There's that Torres spirit," Dad said. There was a pause. "Actually, I guess I'm that Torres spirit. Get it? I'm a spirit, and my name is Torres? Torres spirit?" He flashed me a goofy grin I remembered well from my childhood, and I groaned.

"*Dad.*"

He laughed. "Anyway, let's give it a try."

"What exactly are we trying?"

"You're going to change the dreamscape. For example, maybe this isn't what you want to be dreaming about. Maybe you want to dream about climbing a mountain or relaxing at the beach or something instead. How do you think you'd make that happen?"

"Um. I guess I'd think about what I want to happen?"

Dad gave my shoulder an encouraging pat. "Good. Good first step. But it's not just about thinking, it's about believing. You have to believe it's going to work, and it will."

I eyed him doubtfully. "So, it's about confidence?"

"Exactly."

"Yeah, I've never been good at confidence."

"Well, this is a good chance to practice, then. Look, we'll start small. Think of something small you want to change about the dreamscape. Maybe you want the walls a different color, or you want it to be night instead of day—anything at all. Think about it and then *believe* it until it happens."

I frowned but closed my eyes, which was weird in a dream but nonetheless something I needed to do to concentrate. My mind had gone annoyingly blank, and I couldn't think of anything I wanted to change. I opened my eyes again in search of inspiration, and at the sight of Robbie, Jackson, and Mr. Raines sitting in front of me, I realized what I wanted to see. But maybe it was too big, too much for my first try…

"Just try it." Dad's voice was soft but encouraging. "What have you got to lose?"

Aside from my father, returned from the grave to give me dreaming lessons? Nothing.

I closed my eyes again and tried to picture them. Mom, Jasmine, Eleanor, Maribel, Eliza. My family, sitting here with my friends and my teacher, seeing me for who I was and supporting me even so. That was what I wanted. That was my dream. I imagined the five of them standing around me, smiling and calling me "Leo," finally recognizing the guy staring out at them from my face. For a second, it seemed to be working. I felt them flickering into being in the dreamscape, becoming real—but then the dark little voice in my head started whispering about how this was stupid because they were never going to accept me, they were never going to see anything but a girl and imagining anything different, even in the safety of the dreamscape, was just setting myself up for disappointment.

Dad breathed a quiet sigh, and I opened my eyes. Not only had my family not appeared, but Jackson, Robbie, and Mr. Raines had vanished, their "LEO LEO HE'S OUR MAN" banners fluttering limply to the ground at my feet. I stood in a classroom with three empty chairs, alone except for the dream-ghost of my dad.

"You almost had it," he said. "What happened there?"

Failure weighed down my shoulders. "I guess I just couldn't believe it. I couldn't believe they would really be here and, you know... Accept me."

Dad smiled gently as he rested his hand on my shoulder. "It's not them you have to believe in. It's yourself."

I made a face. "Ugh, Dad, that's so cheesy."

"Doesn't change the fact that it's true. Anyway, don't worry. You'll get this. And after you've mastered it, you'll be ready to start learning how to walk into other people's dreams."

"I don't know if I can—I'll be ready to *what*?"

Dad laughed, but it was like there was a sunburst behind him, a bright light glaring through the dream and melting it away like morning fog.

"Looks like you're waking up." The light traced the edges of his body so brightly I could no longer make out the details, just a Dad-shaped outline in the dreamscape. "See you next time. Leo."

I started awake with a snort to find I'd been sleeping with my head pillowed on my arms on the library study desk. Jackson sat across from me reading a comic book, his dark eyes and raised eyebrow just visible above the glossy cover.

"Nice nap?"

I ran a hand across my face, trying to push away the disoriented sleepy feeling. "I didn't sleep so well last night."

Jackson's expression softened, and he nodded with understanding before going back to his comics.

There were only a few minutes left in study hall, so I spent the rest of the time gazing out Mr. Raines' favorite window and thinking quiet thoughts about dreams, my dad, and how good it had felt to hear him call me "Leo," even if it probably hadn't been real.

When the bell rang, we headed for the cafeteria at a faster pace than Jackson's usual leisurely stroll. Getting to the lunch line early was paramount unless you wanted to be waiting around for half the lunch period—plus, by the time you got your food, it'd be the gross bits scraped from the bottom of the pan and there wouldn't be any good seats left, so it was just better all around to get to lunch early.

We hustled through the double doors and found only a small line snaking back from where the lunch ladies stood doling out scoops of beige and brown. My packed lunch and I got in line with Jackson for moral support, and we managed to get in and out in about five minutes—not bad at all. Our favorite table by the windows was free, and I found myself dropping my backpack onto the table next to me instead of on the floor. Jackson gave it an odd look but shrugged and dug into his plate of beige, and I tried to devote the same attention to my own, much more appetizing lunch of leftover rice with lentils and mushrooms, but my gaze kept wandering around the cafeteria.

Finally, I caught a glimpse of reddish-blond curls, an uncertain figure holding a tray and glancing uneasily around the lunchroom. I raised a hand and gestured to the empty seat next to me, guarded by my backpack. Robbie gave a relieved flash of a grin and strode over to sit beside me.

Jackson slowly laid down his fork and looked from me to Robbie and back again. He was frowning, not in a disapproving or judgmental way, just in a *what exactly is going on here* sort of way.

"So, Jackson," I said. "This is Robbie. Robbie, Jackson."

Jackson gave a curt little nod that Robbie reflected back at him, and there was an awkward silence. I wanted to explain to Jackson that Robbie was trans, Robbie had saved me when I was drowning in panic in the hallway, but I didn't want to out Robbie without his permission, especially since it sounded like maybe he was one of the stealth trans guys he'd been talking about earlier. Plus, I felt like putting the whole rescue thing into words would lessen it somehow.

So instead, I said, "Robbie's in my Geometry class. And Social Studies."

"Mm." Jackson still looked wary, casting Robbie appraising glances between bites.

"Are you the friend who's into death metal?" Robbie asked.

"Yeah." He did not say *I'm the only friend*, which I appreciated.

"He's also the one who helped me this morning," I told Robbie. "With my—" I gestured subtly toward my binder. "—problem."

"Oh!" Robbie grinned at Jackson. To my surprise, he continued, "I told him he should get a zip-up binder like the one I have. It's a lot easier to get on and off."

Something changed in Jackson's eyes, and the wariness relaxed into understanding. "They make zip-up ones?"

"Yeah, they're great."

"Well, that would've saved us a lot of trouble this morning, wouldn't it?" Jackson threw a pointed look in my direction. "Maybe toss out the death harness and invest in one you can actually get on without dislocating something?"

I bristled. "Hey, I spent money on this thing! I'm not gonna just throw it away and get another one. It's the principle of the thing."

Jackson snorted into his soda. "Yeah, it's always 'the principle of the thing' with you, isn't it? Just like with that damn skateboard..."

"Do *not*," I said, but Jackson was already smirking and telling Robbie about the skateboard I'd bought second-hand on the internet and how it had arrived with three wheels, only two of which worked with any reliability. I'd still determinedly taken it outside and tried to skate on it, but then all three wheels had jerked to a halt at the same instant and sent me hurtling to the pavement. One harried ride to the hospital and four stitches in my chin later, and Jackson, the doctor, and every member of my family were entreating me to throw out the skateboard and possibly burn it in a sacrificial fire.

And okay, so riding the thing hadn't been my brightest move, but I hadn't actually told Jackson—or anyone—the truth about why I'd wanted the skateboard so badly in the first place. There'd been this guy in a book I was reading, and he'd just been so freaking cool, everything I wanted to be, and he'd been a skateboarder. Back then, I hadn't understood the twinge in my chest when I read about him—I'd figured I just had a crush on him or something—but when I saw a used skateboard for sale, that twinge had turned into a bone-deep ache and I'd *needed* to buy it. And if I'd maybe also picked up an old jean jacket at the thrift store that looked a lot like the one the guy wore on the front cover of the book, well, that didn't mean anything, right? And then the skateboard had pitched me off into a world of pain, and I'd quietly dropped the jean jacket in the donation bin outside the thrift store and thrown the skateboard into the back of my closet to get dusty.

At no point during the experience had it occurred to me that the thing that hurt worst wasn't my face hitting the pavement, but the fact that I could never really be that cool skateboarder guy from the book. Or any of the guys I read about or wrote about or watched in anime or movies or on TV. It didn't matter what jacket I wore or whether I had a skateboard or not. I could never be like them. And that knowledge had burrowed its way inside my chest and itched for years, and it was only now that it was finally starting to fade.

We were about halfway through lunch and Jackson was singing a few bars of his most recent favorite song to Robbie, who was actually listening attentively instead of running for the hills, when I felt a tap on my shoulder.

It was the new girl from first period—Maya something. Being new, she probably hadn't known about the get-to-lunch early rule, because she'd apparently just broken free of the lunch line and had some depressing scoops of food-ish mush on her plate.

"Hey, do you guys mind if I sit with you?" She cast a glance over her shoulder, and I followed her gaze to the table where Aspen, Carly, and a bunch of other popular girls sat. And while Maya had seemed pretty chummy with Aspen and co. that morning, now Aspen was shooting her a dirty look that burned all the way across the cafeteria.

The seat on my other side was empty, so I scooted my tray closer to Robbie's. "Sure, go ahead."

Maya slid into the seat, and I took a second to notice her as I hadn't when I'd been panicked and cornered in the classroom that morning. She had long, straight black hair that hung past her shoulders, and her warm brown skin was smoothed by light touches of makeup. While she wore the same kind of snug top and skirt as my sister and the other popular girls in our school, she moved in it like it didn't quite fit, or like she wished she could be wearing something else.

"Sorry about this morning, by the way," Maya said, and I nearly dropped my fork in surprise. "I guess we kind of cornered you, but Aspen and Carly wanted to talk to you, and I went along because—I don't know, I kind of wanted to talk to you too, but not like that."

I frowned but managed an uncaring shrug. "No big deal. Don't worry about it." Aspen's laser eye was still boring into the back of my neck, so I asked, "Are you and Aspen friends?"

Maya was trying unsuccessfully to poke her straw into her juice box, a motion that got fractionally more violent as she glanced back at Aspen. "I don't think so. I don't really want to be, anyway. She seemed nice at first, but I don't think she is."

"Good guess." Jackson took the juice box wordlessly from Maya and inserted the straw with an expert jab. Maya's eyebrows lifted in surprise as he handed it back to her, and then she nodded her thanks and took a sip.

"So, you're from that charter school, right?" Jackson said. "Like Robbie?"

Maya cast an uncertain glance in Robbie's direction. "Yeah. It wasn't a big school, but it was nice, you know? Everybody knew each other."

Robbie was studying his plate with sudden intense concentration but wasn't actually eating anything. Jackson caught my eye and glanced from Robbie to Maya. I shrugged.

"I guess this must be pretty different, then," I said.

Maya laughed. "Yeah, it really is. I mean, not in a bad way. But just...yeah. Different."

We fell into another awkward silence, and then Jackson perked up as he realized he now had two people at this table who didn't yet know the true glory of his favorite kind of music. He launched into a treatise on the merits of death metal while I poked at the remains of my lunch and tried to decipher the weirdness between Maya and Robbie. If everyone had known each other at their old school, it stood to reason they'd known each other, too, but there was definite awkwardness there. Failed friendship? Failed more-than-friendship?

I cast a covert look at Robbie. He was eating now, slowly, and was even looking up from his plate from time to time at Jackson's animated discussion. I nudged him gently with my shoulder. "You okay?"

Robbie glanced at me in surprise and gave a flicker of a smile. "Yeah, I'm fine."

I eyed him doubtfully, though he seemed to mean it. A glance back at Maya showed her laughing as Jackson imitated an electric guitar with some very convincing "wreow, wreow, wreow" noises.

Robbie was watching Maya, too, a faint frown furrowing his brow. I raised a questioning eyebrow at him and he sighed.

"I'll tell you later." His breath was warm on my cheek, and I realized how close we were sitting, close enough for me to see the little flecks of lighter brown in the irises of his dark eyes. "Promise."

We finished our lunches and headed to class together, discovering along the way that all four of us had Gym, then split up for the period after that, then ended up together again with Choir last period. Gym was the class I'd been dreading the most, but I figured I'd just have to deal with it.

It wasn't until we got there that I realized: There was one unisex bathroom, and two trans guys who didn't dare go into the gendered locker rooms to change. As Maya headed for the girls' locker room and Jackson for the guys', Robbie and I lingered outside the closed door of the only safe bathroom in the school.

"You want to go in first?" I asked.

Robbie was already settling down on the floor of the hallway and leaning his back against the wall. "You go ahead." He offered a wincing smile. "I'm not in any rush."

I got changed as quickly as I could, trading in my comfortable layers for a loose, dark gray T-shirt and gym shorts. The binder stayed on, because no way in hell was I taking it off. The shorts were loose enough and long enough to kind of hide the shape of my thighs, but I still felt self-conscious seeing my bare legs stretching down to my sneakers. They were lightly dusted with hair but nowhere near as furry as Jackson's or the other guys' in our class, and there was something a little too shapely about them. Jasmine had always said I was lucky to have such nice legs, and there'd even been a pervy old man after church one week who'd drawn me aside for the sole purpose of telling me how nice they were. It still made my skin crawl when I thought about it.

But Robbie was waiting patiently outside for his turn in the bathroom and gym class was starting in five minutes, so I pushed away my insecurities and zipped up my bag.

"All yours," I said as I opened the bathroom door. The air of the hallway was cool on my bare legs, and I felt nervous and underdressed.

Robbie brushed past me looking pale but determined, and I knew he was just as scared as I was.

Chapter Six

Ms. Yamaguchi accepted the note I handed her and scanned it with a quick, business-like sweep of her brown eyes. Her short, spiky white hair didn't budge as she gave a curt nod. "Got it. Head over to the boys' side, Torres."

The ease of it took my breath away, especially since my third period teacher, Ms. Rawling, had frowned at my note for a solid twenty seconds and then completely ignored my existence for the rest of class. She hadn't called on me, hadn't referred to me, hadn't even glanced in my direction, and she'd marked me present in her gradebook without ever calling my name. Ms. Hernández had told me the teachers all received some kind of training over the summer about dealing with gender-nonconforming students, and any purposeful deadnaming or misgendering would supposedly result in a backlash from the administration.

I had my doubts about how effective the administration would be in enforcing that particular rule, but maybe Ms. Rawling figured she could avoid the issue altogether by just pretending I didn't exist. And honestly, if it was either being ignored or being referred to by the wrong name and gender for the rest of the year, I'd much rather be ignored.

Pushing aside thoughts of possibly transphobic teachers, I jogged over to where Jackson, Robbie, and the other guys in our class were stretching, some talking and laughing together, some gazing tiredly ahead in an after-lunch stupor. A few glanced at me as I joined the group, and one or two gave me the cool-guy nod, a little upward jerk of the chin that said, *S'up, dude.* I returned it as best I could as a non-native speaker and went to stretch by Jackson and Robbie. Across the room, Maya was stretching on her own while Aspen and her royal court laughed and ignored her from a few feet away. She looked lonely and I wished she could've come to join us, but gym class was the one place where gender segregation was still the law of the land. I was just glad to have been segregated on the right side of the gym.

Jackson sidled up to me and followed my gaze to Maya. "She seems cool."

"She does." I hesitated. "I think maybe she was flirting with me in first period."

Jackson gave me an appraising look but didn't reply, and I remembered the smile on Maya's face, the lilt in her voice when she'd asked me my name.

She hadn't seemed particularly flirty at lunch, but I'd been a little occupied with Robbie's nearness and the general anxiety of hoping Jackson got along with these new people I'd picked up over the course of the morning. And then there was the big question: Did Maya know about me? She hadn't seemed to, but for all I knew she'd pegged me from the first moment, or maybe word had already gotten around and she was just being nice to the poor trans kid. I didn't even know how I felt about her, just that she seemed nice enough and there was a hint of something *more* behind her brown eyes, something that made me wonder what was hiding under her careful makeup and smiles.

"All right, finish stretching and line up for drills!" Ms. Yamaguchi shouted.

As always, I was surprised by the volume a petite 65-year-old was capable of, but Ms. Yamaguchi had never seemed bothered by the limitations of her stature or her age. Her wiry biceps flexed impressively as she closed the gym doors, and as our sneakers squeaked on the shiny gym floor, I thought about the time I'd seen her in the weight room lifting ludicrously large barbells while a bunch of buff senior guys looked on in awe.

Gym class wasn't too bad, maybe Yamaguchi going easy on us since it was the first day of school, but it was definitely a challenge with my binder on. Sweat collected itchily under it after just a few dashes back and forth across the gym, and the inability to draw in a really deep breath slowed me down, leaving me toward the back of the pack of running guys instead of solidly in the middle as I would've been otherwise. Robbie seemed to be struggling, too, though I saw him fiddle with the zipper of his binder once or twice, and he looked more comfortable after. Just as I was thinking grimly that maybe I would need to invest in a zip-up after all, Yamaguchi waved us through an obstacle course of bright orange cones and over to the bleachers to take a breather while the girls had their turn.

On the guys' side of the gym, there was a lot of leaning over with hands on thighs, high fives being exchanged and towels rubbed across damp brows. The scent of guy sweat filled the air without apology, and I realized I was jealous of these sweaty, hairy guys with their cracking voices and oily faces. I didn't want that, but I *wanted that.*

Jackson tossed a towel at my face; I caught it smoothly and used it to wipe my forehead. We'd been told to bring water bottles, and I was glad of it now. I settled down by Jackson on the bleachers and poured cool liquid down my throat, and Robbie flopped down next to me looking wilted but otherwise okay. I watched his throat move as he took a gulp from his water bottle, then shifted my gaze away to safer things.

Maya, I was pleased to see, was hands-down the fastest runner of the girls, leaving Aspen and her cronies in the dust and looking very much at home in her white gym shirt, red shorts, and sneakers, her long black hair flapping behind her in a high ponytail. Her legs moved smoothly and powerfully as she ran, and there was an easy confidence to her I hadn't seen before. Ms. Yamaguchi was watching her too, a calculating smile on her face.

"Maya better watch out," Jackson said. "Yamaguchi'll have her on the track team before dinnertime."

"You really think she'll wait that long?" I asked.

Jackson grinned, and we watched the girls run in silence. It was weird to think that last year I'd been there among them, feeling like something wasn't right but unable to tell what it was.

I realized abruptly that Robbie hadn't said anything since he'd sat down, and I glanced over to find him also watching Maya, though the look on his face was pinched, like just looking at her hurt him.

He caught me looking and threw me a weak smile, but he didn't give any explanation, so I didn't push. I knew what it was like to have secrets that hurt you. He'd tell me in his own time or not at all, and that was just fine.

Robbie and I had English next, so we said a temporary farewell to Maya and Jackson and started the long hike to the opposite end of the building. Without Jackson and Maya to keep the conversation flowing, we fell into silence, the curse of two introverts finding themselves alone together.

"So, uh, how do you like the school so far?" I asked, then winced and wished I'd asked something less stupid-sounding. *How's school?* was what relatives asked when they didn't know what else to say, and I always hated it when they did, mostly because I was never sure how to answer.

Robbie didn't seem to mind the question, though. He shot me a small smile and hugged his English textbook closer to his chest. "It's pretty all right so far, actually." His dark eyes flickered over to meet mine, and heat rushed to my cheeks as I hurriedly looked away.

"Did you like your old school?" *Idiot, stop asking about school. Ask about what music he likes or video games or something, anything but stupid school!*

"It was okay." He made a face and gave a quick bark of a laugh. "Actually, no, that's a lie. To be honest, I pretty much hated it."

"Why? I mean, if you want to talk about it. Really, it's none of my business. Sorry, I shouldn't have even asked—"

Robbie arched an amused eyebrow at me. "Do you always apologize before you've even offended someone?"

"I mean, I guess it saves time?" I glanced at him and we both laughed. "So, I didn't then? Offend you."

"Not so far." He drew in a breath and let it seep out slowly through his lips. "It's hard for me to make friends. I'm not good at talking to people, or knowing what to say when they talk to me. I like drawing a lot better than dealing with people, really. If I could sit in a room and draw all day without ever having to deal with anyone, that'd pretty much be my idea of a perfect day. But when you don't know how to talk to people and you sit around drawing in your notebook all the time, people tend to think you're kind of weird."

This was where I should assure him he wasn't weird, but instead I said, "What's wrong with weird?"

Robbie grinned. "Nothing. I like weird. But there aren't a ton of people lining up to be friends with the weird trans kid."

Our steps had slowed to a crawl. We were probably going to be late for English, but I didn't care in the least if we were. "Were you out, then? At your last school."

A shadow passed over Robbie's face. "I was, yeah. Just at the end. I guess it didn't really change how people treated me all that much. The ones who ignored me still ignored me, and the ones who didn't ignore me still didn't, they just had different words to throw at me."

"Jeez, I'm sorry. That sucks."

It wasn't much in the way of comfort, but Robbie smiled like I'd said the exact right thing. We walked on in silence for a few steps.

"Can I see your drawings sometime?" I asked.

His gaze dropped to the floor, an honest-to-goodness blush rising in his cheeks. "Yeah, I mean, if you want to. Most of the ones I do at school are just doodles, but they make me feel steadier, you know? If I'm anxious about something, drawing helps ground me."

"Maybe I should try that."

Robbie shrugged. "People deal with anxiety in different ways."

"My way is letting it totally bowl me over and then hiding in the bathroom and hyperventilating for a while."

"I mean, that's an option," Robbie said with a wry lift of an eyebrow. "Or you could try breathing exercises, or doing something physical like taking a walk, or listening to a certain song, or really doing anything to ground yourself in the moment instead of in your panic."

"Grounding myself," I said uncertainly.

Robbie leaned his back against the nearest locker to look at me. "Yeah, it basically just means focusing on what your body is feeling instead of what's going through your head. Like right now, I can feel the lockers against my back, and the floor under my feet, and the textbook I'm holding, and my backpack on my shoulders—stuff like that. And if there's someone around who knows what's happening, someone you trust, they can sometimes help. They can kind of be your anchor."

The bell echoed from the speakers overhead, but for the

second time that day, I ignored it and focused on Robbie. "How?"

The hallway around us was empty, everyone else already safe in their classes behind closed doors, so no one was there to see it when Robbie reached out and took hold of my hand. Electricity jolted up my arm, and my fingers thrummed with the warmth of his skin on mine.

"Like this." His expression was calm, and there was an earnestness in his eyes that made the breath catch in my throat. "When you're in a panic, it's like you're trapped in your own head, right? It's hard to break out of that, but focusing on something physical, or something outside of yourself, can help."

My mouth was dry. "So, I would focus on your, um. On your hand?" I remembered his hand wrapping over mine in the empty classroom, squeezing a gentle rhythm against my fingers. This was what he'd been doing for me then, wasn't it? Grounding me against the panic.

"Yeah," Robbie said. "Like, what does it feel like where I'm touching you? What is your body feeling right now?"

A nervous thrill went through me, and I knew I absolutely could not tell him what my body was feeling at that moment. "Uh, I mean, your fingers are—they're warm. And, uh…"

Robbie laughed. "You don't have to say it out loud. Just think about it." He gave my hand a quick squeeze and let go, and I was surprised by how empty my fingers felt afterward. "Anyway, that's one technique. I learned a bunch of them from my therapist. I can tell you some more sometime, if you want."

"Yeah, definitely." Did my voice sound as breathless as I felt? I grasped for words, any words, and said the first ones that came into my head. "I guess I kind of use my writing like you use your drawing, now that I think about it."

Robbie tilted his head, a small smile pulling at his lips. "You write?"

I averted my eyes and shoved my hands into my pockets, my cheeks warming. "Stories, yeah. They're not very good, but I've always liked to read, and sometimes I get frustrated because things in books don't go the way I want them to, so I started… You know. Writing my own stories. I do it a lot when I'm not feeling great, and it always—It's a good escape."

Robbie's smile softened. "I know exactly what you mean."

He opened his mouth again, and I was afraid he was going to ask to see one of my stories, so I blurted out, "We should probably get to class." I nodded at the clock, which showed it was a full two minutes past when we should've been in English class.

Robbie's eyes widened. "Oh, crap, I didn't even—sorry. I'm not the best at keeping track of time."

We skidded into English class almost four minutes late, but by some miracle, Mr. Brutlag had been detained at the principal's office and didn't stroll in until a minute or so after Robbie and I slouched into two empty seats at the back of the room. Mr. Brutlag spent a few moments sharing his amused irritation that (a) the principal's office was so far from his classroom, and (b) said principal had demanded to see him during the five-minute break, thus requiring him to cross the entire length of the building twice and also ensuring he would be late getting back to class. Maybe because he was so late, he didn't even bother to read the roll, just gave the room a quick scan for any empty desks and marked everyone present, which was good since I'd completely forgotten to hand him one of the notes Ms. Hernández had given me.

Class wasn't bad, mostly just Mr. Brutlag talking about what we'd be doing that semester with his usual friendly dry humor, but I found it especially hard to pay attention, my gaze invariably wandering to Robbie. The only other free seat had been diagonally in front of mine, so I was able to look at him without him knowing he was the object of my attention. His head was bent over his desk, reddish-blond curls hiding his face, but his pencil twitched back and forth over his notebook. The movements of his hand were quick and confident, and when I craned my neck a little, I could see he was drawing a series of interlocking shapes that seemed random but nonetheless fit together in a weirdly perfect way.

His whole body seemed to relax as he drew, and while I had the sense he was listening to every word Mr. Brutlag said, it also seemed like Robbie wasn't entirely in class anymore, like he'd ascended to some other plane that allowed him to eavesdrop on our world without being affected by it.

My eyes traced the relaxed curve of his shoulders, the easy, practiced movements of his hand. I realized I was absently stroking my palm where his hand had touched mine and commanded myself to stop it immediately.

God, what was this? I'd had stupid little crushes before, but I'd never felt this all-consuming need to stare at someone in the middle of class. And for all that Robbie had been exceptionally nice to me since we'd met, I didn't even know if he was into guys, let alone me in particular, so why even bother feeling this way? And, hey, maybe it wasn't even a crush at all. Maybe this was just the novelty of having another trans guy so close by, someone I felt a real, genuine connection with.

Sure. That had to be it. I sat up straighter in my chair and tried to focus on what Mr. Brutlag was saying, but it was a losing battle. Thankfully, Robbie never glanced back and caught me staring at him, and when the bell finally rang, I felt like I'd gotten it out of my system and could resume being a functioning human being. And then Robbie got to his feet and tossed me a grin over his shoulder, and my stomach exploded with butterflies.

Oh. Oh, no.

Jackson and Maya met up with us on the way to the choir room, and no longer being alone-alone with Robbie seemed to help. The weird fluttery feelings left my stomach and I settled back into friendship mode, joining in the chatter and banter and just enjoying walking down the hallway with three people I could call my friends. As we drew closer to the choir room, I marveled that my first day at school being seen as a guy had gone so smoothly, and that was a mistake.

Jasmine was sitting in the choir room.

I'd forgotten Choir wasn't separated by grade—the

sound-proofed walls echoed with the voices of ninth graders all the way up to seniors. My sister sat with a group of her friends in the corner, chatting and rolling her eyes at some ninth-grade boys putting on a show of wrestling in front of her. The choir teacher was nowhere in sight, and I kind of wanted not to be in sight, either.

"What is it?" Maya rested a hand on my arm. She'd been keeping pace beside me as Robbie and Jackson strode ahead of us talking about some local band they both knew and liked, and so of course she noticed when I ground to a halt and stared in horror for three full seconds. "What's wrong?"

"My sister," I said.

Maya frowned and followed my gaze, and it was right at that moment that Jasmine spotted us. My heart froze in my chest, because instead of throwing me a cheerful wave like she normally would've done, she got to her feet and stalked over to me, her jaw clenched and her eyes blazing.

"Could I talk to you for a minute?" She didn't even glance at Maya, and before I'd managed to gasp out more than a helpless "Uh," Jasmine had grabbed my arm in a death grip and dragged me out of the choir room and around the corner to the abandoned stretch of hallway between the band room and one of the school's side exits.

"All right, what is going on with you?" Jasmine demanded.

I stared at her. My mind was a roaring white wall of stage fright.

"People have been coming up to me all day and asking if I have a brother, and I finally figured out they meant you.

And I can see why. Jeez, look at you—and your hair! Mom is gonna freak. And what are Gram and Gramps going to say?"

There was a lot to deal with in those few sentences, but somehow the words that came out of my mouth were, "What did you tell them?"

"What?"

"When people asked if you had a brother. What did you tell them?"

"I said no," Jasmine nearly exploded, "because I *don't.* All I have is my weird sister who is, I don't know, cosplaying or something and swaggering around with a girl on her arm. Are you gay? Is that it? Is that what this is?"

I should've been hurt, shamed, diminished, but I felt weirdly like laughing. "No, I'm not gay. Bi or pan, probably, but not gay."

"Then what is going on?"

"I'm a guy," I said. "I'm trans."

Jasmine went silent, a look of such complete and utter shock on her face that I almost did start laughing. I held it in, though, because even in this weird fugue state I was in, I knew it wouldn't have been appropriate.

"You're kidding," she said finally.

"I'm not."

"But—You can't just decide you're a boy and expect everyone to go along with it! That's not how it works!"

I had no idea where this untouchable calm was coming from, but I was glad for it. "I didn't 'decide' I'm a boy. I've always been one. I always knew something was off about me, and I finally realized it's because I'm trans. Look, I have some videos you can watch—"

Jasmine gave an unsteady laugh and backed away from me. Tears shone in her eyes, threatening her mascara. "This is crazy," she said. "You know that, right? This is weird and crazy and I just—I can't right now."

She hurried back down the hall toward the choir room, and I was left standing alone in the hallway, breathing hard and realizing I'd just come out to my sister and it had not, in fact, gone very well at all.

I was somehow not surprised to see Robbie's curly head poke around the corner. From the grim look on his face, he'd heard at least the tail end of my conversation with Jasmine.

"Leo?"

I laughed a little. It sounded unstable even to my own ears. "Well, that could've gone better."

Robbie came toward me cautiously, as if approaching a wounded animal. He didn't say anything, and he was right in front of me when I pressed my hand over my face and the first hot tears stung my eyes. I drew in a choked breath and tried to fight them back, but the tears came anyway, and a warm weight settled onto my shoulder that I realized was Robbie's hand. He held it there silently as I struggled to control myself, and finally I felt steady enough to pull my hand away from my eyes and draw in a shaky breath.

Robbie's lips bent into a faint smile. "You look like hell," he said softly.

I snorted and rubbed my hand over my face again. I'd

seen myself in the mirror plenty of times after I was done crying, so I knew he was probably right.

"I thought I could do this." My voice was small. Miserable. "I thought if I just, if I told them, that they'd be okay with it, and it would all be okay."

"It will be," Robbie said. "Maybe not right away, but it will."

I studied him in the fluorescent lights, aware of the dissonant harmonies of unstable teen voices singing scales down the hall.

"Was it for you?"

Robbie's gaze dropped, and I wondered if I'd been wrong to ask, if I shouldn't have pried. But then he said, "Mostly. It hasn't been perfect, but I'm pretty happy with where I've ended up."

Unspoken between us were the pained looks and awkward silences between him and Maya, the things he'd mentioned about being bullied in his last school. But now wasn't the time to talk about any of that. I sighed and tilted my head toward the choir room. Yet again, Robbie and I were going to be late for class.

"I guess we should…"

"We should," Robbie agreed. He glanced at the exterior door a few feet away from us. "Or…"

I stared at him, uncomprehending, and he smiled and pushed the door open. A warm breeze that smelled like sunshine and earth filled my lungs, and I knew I was going to follow him out into the afternoon. In the mood I was in, I would've followed him anywhere that wasn't a stuffy choir room with my angry little sister in it.

We ended up seated at the base of a tree in the backyard of the school, carefully positioned so as not to be visible from any of the windows. I leaned my back against the rough bark and Robbie sat next to me, close enough for me to feel the heat of his body next to mine. We didn't speak, but somehow it wasn't awkward. The sunlight was warm and so was Robbie's presence beside me, and we sat there in such a comfortable silence that I wouldn't have minded if it never ended.

After only a few minutes, however, I heard feet scuffing softly over the grass, and a glance over my shoulder showed Mr. Raines walking purposely toward us. We'd had to walk past the windows of the library to get here, and he'd probably seen us before we'd tucked ourselves out of sight behind the tree.

"Crap," I said.

"Hello to you, too, Leo." Mr. Raines sounded amused. "Might I ask what has driven you and Mr. Welsh out into the yard, aside from this beautiful weather?"

"My sister," I said in a dark voice, and Mr. Raines winced.

"Ah."

I waited for him to kindly tell us to go back to class, but he lowered himself cross-legged onto the grass in front of us. His green suit jacket had been folded over his forearm, and now he dropped it onto the grass and let it blend into the greenness there.

I remembered what Robbie had said about not being good with people and wondered how he felt about this development. He was plucking blades of grass from the ground, his gaze fixed on the motion of his fingers, and I knew he was wishing he had his notebook handy as the silence stretched between us and Mr. Raines. Finally, Mr. Raines leaned back on his long, lanky arms and gazed up at the blue, blue sky above us.

"You know," he said slowly, "my family didn't react well at all when I told them I'd fallen in love with a man."

Something jolted in my chest. I'd known dimly that Mr. Raines was one of the advisors of the school's Gay Straight Alliance, but somehow it had never occurred to me that he fell on the gay side rather than the straight. I glanced at Robbie. His fingers had stilled over the blades of grass, and his eyes were wide and fixed on Mr. Raines' face.

"It was many years ago, of course," Mr. Raines went on in his usual calm tones. "People were less accepting then. Some of them still are. Out of everyone, though, my father took the longest to understand. There was a time when I thought he would never be able to accept me, that this was the end of our relationship and I was just going to have to get used to him not being in my life. But on the day of my wedding, he showed up. He didn't look happy, but he was there. He watched me pledge my life to the man I loved, and I think he understood a little. Not as much as I wanted, but enough."

The breeze rustled the leaves overhead, and Robbie spoke into the silence.

"Are you still okay? You and your dad."

Mr. Raines gave a soft, sad smile. "He died a few years ago. But before he died? Yes. We were okay. He even gave Leo and me an anniversary present."

Another jolt in my chest. "Leo?"

Mr. Raines grinned. "I told you I liked the name."

He got to his feet, gathering up his suit jacket and brushing some bits of grass and a few friendly ants from the fabric. "I hope this isn't going to become a trend, skipping class like this?"

"No," I said, at the same time Robbie said firmly, "No, sir."

"Good. I'll leave you boys to it, then." He headed back to the school building, and Robbie and I were left in the perfect afternoon sunlight with nothing to do but close our eyes and enjoy it.

Chapter Seven

I'd half expected Jasmine to be waiting at Jackson's car, ready for another confrontation. As I stepped out into the school parking lot, though, I saw her piling onto the bus with a few of her friends. The bus had pulled out by the time Jackson came loping over to the Toyota, a cautious look on his face as he spotted me leaning against the side of his car with my arms folded.

"Uh, so, you kinda disappeared there, my dude," he said.

"Yeah. Sorry. I told Jasmine and she freaked out, and so I kind of just didn't go back to class after. I sat outside instead."

Jackson winced appropriately and shot me another cautious look. "Just you, all by yourself?"

"And Robbie." I could've added, *And Mr. Raines, who is gay and married to a man named Leo, apparently*, but that felt like a step too far.

"And Robbie," Jackson echoed. It was hard to decipher his tone, but before I could figure out if he was mad or not, he shrugged and went to unlock the driver's side of the Toyota. "I'm guessing we're not playing chauffeur, then?"

"You guess right."

After I'd flopped into my seat and pulled on my seatbelt, I leaned my head back against the headrest and closed my eyes. "Jackson, I'm probably never going to say this again, but I think I'd really like to hear some Korean death metal right now."

"What, seriously?" The disbelief in his tone couldn't hide his excitement. "'Cuz I just got this new album—"

"Play it," I said. "As loud as you want."

I cracked an eye to find Jackson grinning like a madman, and soon we were speeding down the road in a screaming flood of bass and electric guitars and voices shouting words I didn't understand but also deeply, deeply understood. The bass pulsed in my chest like an extra heartbeat, and while I didn't ordinarily like that, today I did. I vanished into the music and even head-banged a little with Jackson at the stoplights, and we took the long way home so we could listen to the full spectacular seventeen minutes of the song. By the time we pulled into the little road leading to my neighborhood, I felt almost normal again. My ears were ringing and I wasn't sure English would come out of my mouth the next time I opened it, but I definitely felt better.

Jackson cranked the volume down to normal levels as we pulled onto my street. A row of neatly trimmed lawns and cookie cutter houses coasted by—white with red shutters, white with blue shutters, white with green shutters—and I realized there was no escaping what was going to come next, which was me walking into my house and telling my family I wasn't the person they'd always thought I was.

Jackson and I sat in my driveway with the engine idling for a full thirty seconds before I undid my seatbelt.

"You gonna be okay?" Real concern wavered in his voice. "'Cuz we can go around the block a few more times if you're not ready. Or, hell, how far is it to the Mexican border? I bet we can be there in two, three days tops, and I hear the food is super cheap…"

I looked at him and thought about how he'd accepted my trans guy status unquestionably the second I'd told him, how he'd started peppering his speech with "my dude"s and "my man"s from that moment onward. How he was the first one who'd ever called me "Leo," and how right it had felt from the very start. He'd bought me my first binder and had it shipped to the house of his semi-hysterical mother and aggressively evangelical father, and he'd even been willing to mildly traumatize himself untangling me from said binder when I'd managed to get myself stuck in it. He was the best friend I'd ever had, and I could never repay him for all he'd done for me.

I considered hugging him, but instead I reached over and gripped his arm. He glanced down at my hand and then covered it with his.

We didn't say anything, being two manly dudes doing a simple manly hand grip in the front seat of an old Toyota, but emotion welled in Jackson's dark eyes, and I knew mine were probably shining with something similar.

"Text me," he said as I opened the car door. "Let me know you're okay."

"I will."

I watched him drive away, then took a deep breath and started up the walk.

I opened the front door to the echoes of laughter and voices. Frowning, I dropped my backpack on the floor of the entryway and followed the sound, a journey that ended with me standing motionless in the living room doorway.

No one noticed me at first, which was good since I needed a few seconds to collect myself. I'd known family was coming in for my birthday, but I hadn't expected them to be here *already*, and I certainly hadn't expected to see my grandmother, grandfather, aunt, and uncle squished shoulder-to-shoulder on our sofa while Mom poured lemonade and Maribel and Eleanor twirled in an improvised dance routine while everyone watched, indulgently enchanted by two nine-year-olds with matching tutus stretched up over their jeans. Eliza sat quietly on the floor in the corner, only the top of her frizzy dark hair visible behind a sixth grade Social Studies textbook, and Jasmine was perched on the piano stool in a relative-appropriate blue dress with a modest neckline and pleated skirt—and pantyhose, even—smiling politely and looking like she'd never exploded at me in the hallway a few hours earlier.

The dance recital had just finished to thunderous applause when Mom turned and spotted me. Her eyes widened, her gaze flicking up to my hair and then down to my clothes, but she recovered smoothly and ushered me into the room with gushing words about how much everyone had been wanting to see me and how anxious they'd been for me to get home from school and join them—and was I surprised? The "big meeting" she'd had that morning had actually been her going to the airport to meet the plane, and after a two-hour drive and one small adventure in the baggage claim area, she'd driven home with four long-lost relatives in tow.

Grandma Pearl had the same sour lemon expression I remembered from the last time I'd seen her, but I knew not to take it seriously. "It's so good to see you, ___," she said. After a long day of not hearing my deadname, it was disorienting to hear it now, like I'd dreamed the whole day and had now woken up back in my previous, inescapable reality. "Come over here so I can look at you."

Grandpa Earl—the second half of Pearl 'n' Earl, as Dad had always called them—was smiling vacantly but looked happy enough, and he even gave me a warm little nod when his watery blue eyes met mine. Aunt Audrey and Uncle Shel were busy complimenting the twins' ballet routine and didn't seem to be paying attention to me, though Audrey's bright dark eyes flicked over to me a few times, her slender eyebrows lifting in question.

Dread curled in my stomach, but I drew forward until I stood in front of Grandma Pearl.

Rheumy brown eyes stared up at me, and I tried not to fidget—or to just plain run, maybe to call Jackson and tell him Mexico didn't sound like such a bad idea after all.

"Well, now," Grandma Pearl said. "You've certainly grown, haven't you? Last time I saw you, you were, what, eleven or twelve?"

"Twelve."

The Colorado branch of the family hadn't visited much over the years, and only Grandma Pearl and Grandpa Earl had bothered to fly out for Dad's funeral.

"Your hair was longer then." Grandma Pearl eyed my chopped and gelled locks with interest but not judgment. To my horror, she patted my chest with one wrinkly hand. "Looks like not much has changed in this department, but no shame in that! Some of the best women in our family have been flat-chested, and they still managed to get husbands!"

"Mom!" my mom said, and I wondered if it might be possible for me to turn to dust and flutter away through the open window. "Sometimes teen girls feel uncomfortable when their bodies start to develop, and so they dress to hide that fact. It's perfectly natural—" Her eyes found mine, reassuring and full of motherly certainty. "—and nothing at all to be ashamed of."

This would've been a wonderful speech if I were indeed a teen girl suffering from embarrassment about my developing body. As I was a teen boy whose body had insisted on giving him boobs, it was somewhat less effective than Mom probably meant for it to be.

"I, uh, actually have a lot of homework," I said.

Mom gave an understanding smile. "Of course. We'll see you at dinner?"

Her eyes mutely offered apology at Grandma Pearl's comments and hoped I wasn't offended. I tried to reassure her silently that I wasn't, but I could only imagine what our family's comments would be when they figured out what was really going on with me.

As I headed for the door, my eyes met Jasmine's. She was watching me with a faint frown, arms folded and lips twisting. She didn't look angry, but she didn't look particularly forgiving, either. It was more like she was trying to piece together the truth of what I'd told her, or to reconcile the sister she'd always known with the brother who was in front of her now.

I threw her a quick, strained smile and left the room. As I went, Audrey murmured something about "late bloomers" and Mom artfully changed the subject, and then Grandpa said in a loud, cheerful voice, "Nice boy! Who was that?"

I swallowed a semi-hysterical laugh and wondered how I was possibly going to survive an entire week with these people. We'd always planned to have them stay with us—the basement had been furnished a few months earlier for the express purpose of hosting visiting relatives—but I'd figured it would be for a night or two, and then they'd be back on their way to Boulder.

But it was Monday. My birthday was on Sunday. That was almost a full week, and it left me in the precarious position of having to find some way to come out to my mom and sisters while family members who were as good as strangers bumbled around getting in the way and making comments about my flat chest.

Happy birthday to me, I thought, and laughed.

Was it the high, unstable laugh of a madman? Maybe. But it was a lot better than crying, so I figured it was okay.

Chapter Eight

Dinner wasn't awful. I got the impression Mom had told everyone I was "going through something," because no one made any more comments about how I looked, though Grandpa did call me "son" a few times—pass the gravy, would you, son? Mom threw me apologetic glances every time it happened, but I ignored them, because Grandpa was the only one in the whole family who was actually seeing me instead of the fake, flimsy girl image the last fifteen years had programmed them to see.

"So, ___," Audrey said as I dug into my grilled eggplant, "your mom tells us you've stopped eating meat?"

I winced inwardly but managed a polite smile. "Yeah, I don't eat meat, eggs, or dairy anymore."

Audrey maintained eye contact with me as she popped a piece of rib roast into her mouth. "That must mean a lot of extra cooking for your mother."

"Actually," Mom slid in smoothly, "___ does most of her own cooking. And the rest of us are trying to cut back on meat, too. There's a lot of science to support that it's healthier for us, and of course it's better for the environment. And the animals."

Audrey gave a merry laugh that made me think of tinkling champagne glasses. "Oh, Dara, you've always been such a free spirit. I doubt the animals mind."

I gave Audrey a flat look. "You don't think animals mind being killed and eaten?"

"Well, of course not," Audrey said. "They're *animals*. That's what they're here for, isn't it?"

I took a deep breath and did not bring up the fact that Audrey had been showing us pictures of her three tiny dogs all evening, calling them "my babies" and worrying that the expensive dog hotel they were staying at wasn't giving them enough love.

Luckily, Mom was on it, as she always was. "So, Jasmine, we've heard from everyone about their first day at school but you. How was it?"

Oh, jeez. From the vegan frying pan into the transgender fire.

I eyed Jasmine warily, but she just offered Mom a breezy smile. "Oh, it was great. I think I'm gonna drop Choir and take a study hall instead, though."

"Oh, honey, why? You've always been such a great singer."

"I'm just not feeling it this year. And, anyway, I'll need that extra study time if I'm going to stay in AP English this year."

"AP English!" Uncle Shel exclaimed through a mouthful of mashed potatoes. "That's great, Jazzy. Congratulations."

Jasmine, who would rather have been called just about anything other than "Jazzy," shot him a look drier than the Sahara. "Thanks, Uncle Shel."

Shel nodded as if he'd missed the sarcasm—which he probably had—and returned to his food with his usual gusto. He wasn't overweight, but he was a big guy, towering over petite Aunt Audrey and looking like a kindly bear with his lumberjack beard and hairy, muscled arms. Where Audrey was delicate and fashionable, Shel looked like a cartoon of an outdoorsman. He was even wearing thick-soled brown boots and a red plaid shirt straight out of a paper towel commercial, and his skin was the leathery kind of tan you could only get after spending a lot of time working out in the sun.

I liked Uncle Shel. He wasn't the most brilliant guy in the world, but he always meant well, and he'd never been anything but nice to me. Plus, I figured the only way you could live with Audrey was to either have her same cruel, cutting wit or to be the kind of person who completely failed to notice sarcasm. Shel seemed to be the latter.

Mom was still playing damage control by keeping Audrey occupied, asking her questions about the new party planning business she was trying to get off the ground, so I let my gaze wander around our big dining room table. Maribel and Eleanor, seated across from me, were building a broccoli forest in their mashed potatoes and holding a serious murmured conversation about which tree the Broccoli Prince should live in. Eliza, seated next to Maribel, was slowly spooning bites of food into her mouth while staring at something in her lap—a book, I assumed, and I hoped Mom wouldn't catch on until Eliza had at least finished whatever chapter she was on. Her brown eyes were wide under the frames of her round black glasses, and she was mouthing along with the words as she read.

Grandma was attending politely to Audrey's talk about the inherent nobility of the party-planning profession, but her gaze kept wandering to the twins' growing broccoli forest, and her lips twitched out of their usual lemony pucker and into a smile at the sight. Grandpa, meanwhile, was simply smiling and enjoying his meal. I missed the days before his memory had started to go, but at least he seemed happy most of the time. It was more than I could say for the rest of us.

I sighed and took a bite of my own potatoes, which Mom had kindly made with non-dairy milk so I could partake. This was my family, and for all that we weren't close to the Colorado relatives, it was kind of nice to have them here. I was sure Mom was happy to see her parents and her sister again, even if Audrey was a bit much, and Uncle Shel, who worked in construction, had already promised he'd fix some stuff up around the house while he was here.

It was nice they were here, and nice they'd wanted to fly across the country to celebrate my birthday and spend time with us, but there was no way I could be comfortable in my own house as long as they were staying with us. And it was hard to forget I'd set a ticking time bomb into motion this morning by having Ms. Hernández write those notes to my teachers. News of my trans-ness was going to spread, and if it spread to the ears of my mom or my other sisters before the week was out, what was supposed to be a quiet coming out to my immediate family would instead become a torrid exposé filled with biting comments from Audrey and probably well-meaning confusion from everyone else.

Which meant I needed to handle this quietly. I needed to talk to my mom before she heard about it from someone else, and then she would at least be on the job keeping the rest of the family from finding out. Whether she would do that because she accepted me or because she didn't, only time would tell.

"So, did you tell her?"

I sighed as I buckled my seatbelt. I didn't meet Jackson's eyes, preferring to be blinded by the morning sunlight glaring through the windshield.

"No."

"You didn't tell her," Jackson said flatly.

"I didn't tell her."

"Even though telling her is the only way to make sure she doesn't find out from somebody else, and the only way to maybe keep your Colorado fam from finding out."

"You got it."

Jackson shook his head and threw the Toyota into reverse. "I hope you know what you're doing, man."

"I definitely don't," I said.

I'd tried. I'd offered to help my mom wash the dishes after dinner, and there had been so many wide open spaces in our conversation where a quiet confession could've gone, but the words hadn't come. Then Mom and I had gone out to sit on the porch together while Maribel and Eleanor took Grandma, Grandpa, Audrey, and Shel on a tour of their plastic pony collection, but the words hadn't come then, either. And finally, just before bedtime, Mom had slipped into my room and sat down on the edge of my bed and told me she was there if I needed to talk about anything, and *the words still hadn't come.*

I mean, how perfect of an opening did I need? My mother had literally been sitting in front of me asking if I wanted to talk about anything, and all I'd been able to do was squeak out, "No, thanks, I'm good," before fleeing to the bathroom to brush my teeth.

"Hey, uh, how's the binder this morning?" Jackson asked. "You manage to get it on?"

I dragged myself out of my misery with a weak smile. "Yeah, I stretched it out a bunch last night, and this morning I managed to get it on first try."

"Nice. Good going, man. Knew you could do it."

It did feel good to have gotten my binder on without traumatizing my best friend in the process, but my mind just kept cycling back to my complete failure to come out to my mom. What if I could never do it? What if I could never say the words? I was still moping about it when we got to school, but my mood lifted at the sight of a familiar figure sliding a purple ten-speed into the school bike rack. I hopped out of the car and jogged over while Jackson was still gathering his stuff from the backseat.

"Hey," I said, and Maya turned with a smile.

She pulled off her bike helmet—also purple and dotted with stars—and attached the helmet to her bike. Gone were the popular-girl clothes of the previous day that she hadn't seemed comfortable in. Instead, she wore a pair of fitted jeans with frayed patches sewn here and there, a button-down white shirt with a loose brown vest, and a pair of faded white sneakers with little green hearts all over them. Colorful bracelets adorned her arms, and a long golden chain with a black cat charm hung from her neck. Large hoop earrings dangled from her ears, swaying as she moved. Her hair, instead of hanging in carefully straightened sheets, was a full, curly mane that framed her face and spilled down over her shoulders. And even though I'd only just met her, I could tell this was the real Maya, the one who'd been in hiding the day before.

"I love it," I said.

A shy smile touched her face. "You don't think it's too much?"

"Are you kidding? It's awesome. And you look—"

Her glance was almost wary this time. "How do I look?"

"Comfortable." I wasn't sure if that was the word I'd been going for, but it was definitely a word that fit.

Jackson strolled up behind me before I could decipher Maya's reaction. "Hey, Maya, lookin' good! I dig the new style."

"Thanks!" Maya cast a bright smile in Jackson's direction. "It's actually not so new. It's how I dress when I'm at home, and how I used to dress at my old school. I guess I just figured new school, new me, you know? I thought I'd try something different on the first day and see what happened."

"And?" Jackson asked.

"And I realized I'd rather be unpopular me than popular somebody else." She shot me a covert look before swinging her bookbag onto her shoulder and starting toward the school building. "Actually, it's because of you I decided to stop pretending."

I blinked. "Because of me?"

"Yeah. You're brave enough to be yourself, so I should be too, right?"

It hit me, then, and I was surprised by how deflating it was. She knew. She knew I was trans. It was fine that she knew—I'd been planning to tell her, anyway—but it had been kind of nice to live in the delusional fantasy of just being a guy in her eyes instead of a trans guy.

She glanced back at me hurriedly, as if worried she'd offended me. "I mean, I think it's great, what you're doing. You're not worrying about what anybody else thinks, you're just being you, and I think that's amazing."

My stomach plummeted to my shoes. Was it really so amazing? I was just trying to live my life, like anybody else.

I wanted to ask how she'd found out, but I was too afraid she was going to say, *"Oh, I knew the second I saw you. It was obvious,"* or something soul-crushing like that, so instead I just said "Thanks" and hoped someone would change the subject before I sank into the ground and found a new home with the earthworms.

Thankfully, Jackson leaped in with a timely question about English class, and I was able to slip away to my locker without Maya suspecting she'd squished my confidence under her cool green-hearted sneakers.

I grabbed the books I would need for my morning

classes and stuffed them into my backpack, and it wasn't until I closed my locker door that I realized Robbie was standing beside me. I jumped, and he gave an apologetic smile.

"Sorry. You seemed a little preoccupied, so I just waited."

He looked tired, and I wondered if he'd had trouble sleeping. Despite all I had to worry about, I'd slept like the dead the night before, which was probably for the best but nonetheless meant I'd had no dreams about Dad, just a long, empty stretch of restful blackness.

"Sorry," I said. Now we'd both apologized for no reason. "How's it going?"

"I feel like I should be asking you that." He lowered his voice. "How's everything with your sister?"

I sighed and leaned my back against the lockers. Down the hall, Maya and Jackson were still talking, Jackson looking animated and Maya laughing at whatever he was saying. I had no idea where Jasmine was, but I assumed she would make sure it was far away from me. She hadn't even looked at me this morning—she'd swept into the kitchen, grabbed a granola bar from the cabinet, and swept out to go catch the bus.

"I don't know," I said. "She hasn't said a word to me since yesterday. I guess the good news is I don't think she's told my mom or anybody about me, but that doesn't mean she won't."

"Maybe you ought to tell them first," Robbie said.

"Oh, I definitely should. But I can't."

"Why not?"

Frustration burned through me again. "I keep trying, but I just can't do it. I open my mouth and the words just don't come out." I eyed him carefully. "I hope you don't mind me asking, but how'd you tell your family?"

Robbie's gaze dropped to his sneakers. "I didn't, actually. My mom found my search history and then went digging around in my room until she found my binders and stuff, and then she told my dad, and it all just kind of exploded from there."

I squeezed my eyes shut, trying to imagine how awful that must've been. "Man, I'm sorry."

"It wasn't how I wanted it to happen, but at least it got things out in the open."

"And were your parents… Were they okay, after a while?"

"I think they finally accepted they weren't going to change my mind," Robbie said, a careful non-answer to my question. "Anyway, I haven't seen them in a while. I live with my aunt now."

The lightness to the words hid devastation beneath, and I realized with a crushing weight in my chest that Robbie's parents had thrown him out, that he was living with his aunt because his actual mother and father couldn't handle having a trans kid under their roof.

He must've seen the anguish in my eyes, because he gave a soft laugh. "It's better this way, honestly. And my aunt's great. She's always been there for me, and I'd much rather be living at her place than stuck at home with people who can't stand me. Better for everybody, right?"

"Jesus Christ, Robbie," I said, and I grabbed hold of him and pulled him into a hug.

He went rigid at the sudden embrace, and I had a heart-stopping moment of wondering what the hell I'd been thinking, grabbing him like that. But he relaxed almost immediately, his tense muscles melting against me, and suddenly all I could feel was the warm weight of his body on mine, the slow in and out of his breathing, the press of his arms against my back. I was consumed by an overwhelming need to hold him like this until a squad of teachers showed up to pry us apart, which is why I let go of him and took an awkward step backward.

"Um. Sorry."

His cheeks were a little flushed, but he gave an easy shrug. "It's okay. I get it. I try not to share my sob story with too many people, because it does tend to cause spontaneous hugging."

I exhaled a nervous laugh and turned toward first period, hoping the movement would clear my head. Robbie settled in beside me, and for all that I wanted to run far away from him, I also desperately wanted him near me. Man, I had it bad.

"Anyway," Robbie said, "I hope this doesn't make you feel weird about coming out to your family, just because mine didn't react all that well. Your mom sounds really cool, and I bet she'll be okay with it."

The funny thing was, I was pretty sure he was right. Mom had always been accepting and wonderful about pretty much everything. She let us dress the way we wanted, she'd let Jasmine experiment with dying her hair and wearing whatever loud combination of makeup she could dream up, and she hadn't batted an eye when I'd cut my hair short. She'd even sat us all down once to make sure we knew that being gay was totally okay and not something we had to hide or be afraid of telling her about. Maribel and Eleanor had shrugged and said "Okay" before heading back upstairs to play, and Eliza had looked relieved but hadn't taken the opening, though I'd seen her doodling "Eliza + Becky" in her notebook on more than one occasion. Maybe she was having trouble getting the words out, too.

When Robbie and I walked into first period, Maya was already there—she gave me a flash of a grin—but so was Aspen.

"Hey, *girl*," she said, a verbal punch to the gut that stopped me in my tracks. "I talked to your sister yesterday. Why are you going around acting like a guy when you're not?"

Everyone in the class was listening, because of course they were. I opened my mouth to say something, anything, but Maya placed herself between Aspen and me without a second of hesitation.

"Look, Aspen, just because you're pissed he's not into you, don't be a jerk."

One of Aspen's perfect eyebrows lifted. "I'm sorry, you think I'm into *that*?"

"You sure were yesterday," Maya said coolly. "What was it you said? That you hoped he didn't have a girlfriend because you were getting tired of the ugly-ass boys in our grade?" She glanced at Carly, standing just behind Aspen, who nodded in confirmation before wilting under Aspen's glare.

The other guys in the class were saying things like "Hey!" and "Who's ugly-ass?" while Maya stared fearlessly at Aspen and Aspen glared back at her with fury in her eyes.

"That was before I knew he was a *she*," she spat.

"He's a he." Maya said it simply and easily, stating a fact. She turned to me. "Leo, are you a he?"

"I'm a he."

"See? I think he would know, right?"

Aspen opened her mouth to say something else, but Mr. Raines entered the room at that moment, and she closed her mouth with a snap.

"Everything all right in here?" His voice was calm, and the carefully blank look on his face suggested he knew exactly what had been going on. He didn't call attention to me by asking me if I was okay, he didn't lecture Aspen on not being a transphobic jerk, he just quietly defused the situation with his presence, for which I was very grateful.

Aspen threw Maya one last glare and returned to her seat, and Robbie nudged me in the direction of my favorite desk in the back row by the windows. I caught a questioning glance from Maya as I moved, a silent *are you okay?*, but I was too shaken to do much more than nod vaguely back at her. There would be time to thank her later. For now, I had to deal with the fact that my secret was out in the open, and I apparently had my sister to thank for it.

Chapter Nine

Maya, Jackson, and Robbie formed an honor guard around me as I walked to and from my classes that day, but I was still very aware of the stares, whispers, and comments as I made my way through the halls. I tried to act like the attention didn't bother me, but it was hard to resist the urge to hide in the nearest janitor's closet until it was time to go home. Luckily, the constant presence of friends around me in the halls and teachers in the classrooms seemed to discourage any outright attacks. I even got a few approving smiles here and there, and an eighth grader I'd never met before ran up to me and gushed about how brave I was until her friends pulled her away.

Aspen, meanwhile, had apparently decided her best course of action was to ignore me completely, which suited me just fine, though the downside was that she was focusing the full weight of her hatred on Maya instead. Her shoulder collided with Maya's as we were walking down the hall to lunch, sending Maya stumbling forward a few steps, and then later as we were doing our stretches in gym class, Aspen declared loudly that she thought it was awful and unfair how some people were put on the track team without even having to try out, while everyone else had to go through grueling two-day tryouts.

Mrs. Yamaguchi, who had entered the gym just in time to hear this, calmly commented, "Run as fast as she does, Jacobs, and you won't have to try out either."

Aspen was left fuming while Jackson and I grinned at Maya from across the room, and even Robbie had a little smile on his face. We'd spent almost the whole day together, much of which had involved Maya's presence, and I still hadn't figured out what was going on between them. Whatever it was did seem to be improving slightly, though. There was still a definite awkwardness between them—and while they talked warmly enough to Jackson and me, they still hadn't said so much as a word to each other—but Robbie didn't look quite so miserable when he looked at Maya.

I found out the answer not from Robbie, as I'd expected, but from Maya.

Just before I'd gone into the unisex bathroom before gym class, Robbie had pulled something from his bag and held it out to me. Frowning, I'd accepted it—and it was a binder, a zip-up one.

"I had an extra one, and I thought you might like to try it out." He averted his eyes from mine, looking oddly shy. "For gym class, I mean. I saw you having some trouble with yours yesterday. This one should be a little bigger on you, too. It's a good idea to go a size up when you're exercising. Makes it a lot easier to do important stuff like breathing."

I thanked him profusely, the gift and the thoughtfulness behind it making the butterflies erupt in my stomach again, and I had to admit the different size and style of binder definitely made gym a lot more tolerable. Before we started our runs, I covertly unzipped it an inch or two through my shirt, and that gave me enough lung capacity to surge forward in the group and actually come in second in our last set of sprints. Pride warmed my chest as I swept past the finish line. The guy who'd won first, a lanky blond kid on the track team, actually grinned and gave me a resounding bro slap on the shoulder to celebrate our shared victory. A simple guy-to-guy interaction that shouldn't have brought tears to my eyes, but I still had to turn away and wipe a hand across my face before I was ready to face the world again.

Yamaguchi rewarded the first and second place winners with a breather while everyone else did more drills, so I was able to sit with Maya on the bleachers for a few minutes and catch my breath.

"Nice job," she said as I sat down beside her.

I uncapped my water bottle and took a much-needed drink. "You, too. Did you do track at your old school?"

She nodded, her dark eyes soft and wistful. "Yeah. I loved it. Like I said before, it was a small school, so we only barely had enough people for the team, and it's not like we ever really won anything, but it was still great. At my first track meet, I was so nervous I didn't place at all, but it was great just to be there and be able to run, you know? My parents and Robbie came and cheered me on, and after the meet they took me out for ice cream even though there really wasn't anything to celebrate—"

"Wait, wait," I said. "Your parents and Robbie came? Like, together?"

An echo of Robbie's pain entered her eyes. "Yeah. I guess he didn't tell you? Robbie's my brother. I mean, not biologically. Our parents started fostering me when I was little, then adopted me a few years later."

"But…your name," I managed through my shock. "Your last one, I mean. It's not—"

"The same as Robbie's? Yeah. I wanted to keep mine. It's the only thing I have left of my birth parents."

I leaned back against the bleachers not sure what to feel. Robbie's parents had found out he was trans and kicked him out, but he wasn't their only child—there was Maya, too, presumably still living with them. How had she taken it when she found out Robbie was trans? She'd stood up for me in front of Aspen, but when it had been her own brother, how had she reacted? Had she done anything or said anything when their parents kicked Robbie out? Things couldn't have gone well between them, or they would be on better terms now. Was this what I had to look forward to with Jasmine?

"Hey, are you okay?" Maya asked.

I swallowed and forced my lips into a weak approximation of a smile. "Fine."

Maya studied my face, a deep line forming between her brows. "Look, I don't know what Robbie's told you about me—"

Yamaguchi shouted for us to get up and rejoin the class before Maya could say more, so I was spared having to figure out how to treat her after this revelation. I jogged back over to join the guys, and soon I had much more to worry about than Maya's possible reaction to Robbie being trans. Ms. Yamaguchi announced that for our cool-down, we were going to be partnering up to do some stretches, and to prevent any "clowning around"—she threw a dark glance at a few of the guys on the basketball team as she said this—she would be choosing our partners. I exchanged a panicked glance with Jackson, hoping Ms. Yamaguchi would be merciful, but I ended up paired with a muscular guy named Otis who I didn't know very well, while Robbie and Jackson somehow got partnered together.

Yamaguchi had Maya help her demonstrate the stretches we were going to do—sitting with our legs outstretched and the soles of our feet pressed together, we were supposed to join hands and then lean backward and forward to stretch out various muscles—and then I was left standing in front of Otis, staring up at his stubbly face and wondering if I was about to die.

Otis gazed back at me silently, and I'd never been so intimidated by anyone in my life. He was in my grade, but the shadow of a beard crept along his chin and up over the strong lines of his jaw. His hair was dark and shaved on the underside and dyed bluish-purple on top, hanging in a floppy swath over one side of his face. To up the intimidation factor even further, he had some kind of vision issue that required him to wear sunglasses even indoors. Only the faint outline of his eyes was visible behind the lenses.

"So," he said in a deep, expressionless voice, "you're the trans guy, right?"

I swallowed. "Uh, yeah."

"Hm." His face was solemn, his voice low. "So if you ever have kids when you get older, I bet they'll have trouble seeing you. Because you'll be...*trans*parent."

I stared at him, uncomprehending, and it wasn't until he burst into a bright, infectious laugh that I realized it was a joke.

"Oh, my God," I said.

Otis grinned, and it transformed his entire face. "Sorry, I couldn't resist. So hey, you want to get started? Yamaguchi's already giving us the evil eye."

I let out a laugh of nervousness mixed with relief and sat down across from him, and Otis chatted companionably with me while we did our stretches. I learned about his girlfriend, who he referred to as his "favorite human," as well as the fact that they were both huge video game nerds and were also two of the straight members of the school's Gay/Straight Alliance.

"You should come to a meeting sometime," Otis said as we did our last few stretches. "There are a lot of cool people there—I mean, *I'm* a member, after all." He laughed again. "But seriously, it's a super welcoming space, and it's good to have people around who are on your side, right?"

I thought about Maya, Jackson, and Robbie in their protective formation around me and knew he was right. I smiled. "Yeah, I'd like that. Fridays at lunchtime, you said?"

"Yep. Just bring your lunch up to room 203—and hey, bring your friends. Everybody's welcome." He threw a glance at two of the basketball guys, who I'd been pointedly ignoring as they made kissing faces at me and mimed having boobs by cupping their hands over their chests. "Well, almost everybody."

Luckily, Ms. Yamaguchi finally noticed what the guys were doing and snapped at them to give her a hundred pushups if they had nothing better to do, but the whole thing still left a bad taste in my mouth.

Otis helped me to my feet and rested a brotherly hand on my shoulder. "There are always going to be idiots," he said. We were standing close enough now that I could see the warmth in the eyes behind his sunglasses. "But the good news is, most people out there aren't. The idiots are just louder."

Choir was after gym, and Jasmine had already made good on her promise to switch to a study hall, so I wouldn't be seeing her there today. Since Robbie and I had missed class the previous day, this unfortunately meant we'd missed the privilege of singing scales for Mr. Tyler in the privacy of his office so he could figure out where to place us in the choir. Rather than allowing us to do that now, he instead had us—along with some other random kid who'd been absent the day before—come down to the piano and, in front of the entire class, sing scales along with his guiding chords.

Robbie sang quietly but well, his face flushed and his gaze fixed on the piano to avoid the many sets of eyes watching us. The other kid wobbled and cracked his way through scales, so much so that even Mr. Tyler was looking apologetic as he listened. Finally, he said, "All right, Torres, you're up next."

I thought of all the voice training videos I'd watched and fought not to think about the eyes watching me. *Just please don't put me in alto*, I thought desperately. I probably was an alto, but no guys were ever assigned to it, and I didn't want to be the first.

I sang my way carefully through the scales. Thankfully I'd neglected to take off the zip-up binder after gym class, and the extra room let me take deeper breaths and hit the lowest pitches I was capable of hitting. I said another silent thanks to Robbie and finished the scales without my voice cracking, and I even found myself thinking there had been a nice richness to my voice as I sang.

Mr. Tyler seemed to think so, too. He nodded approvingly and slid a pencil behind his ear. He was a youngish guy, probably somewhere in his early thirties, with a hipster goatee and thinning brown hair.

"All right, boys," he said. "Welsh and Davis, you're in tenor, and Torres, I'm putting you in baritone. You're on the higher end, but we need baritones, and you've got a nice range and a good steady pitch. And who knows, maybe by the time you're a senior, you'll be ready to join the ranks of our proud basses."

A group of senior guys in the corner pumped their fists and boomed, "Yeah!" in their deep, rumbling voices, and I managed a weak smile. Mr. Tyler had seen the note from Ms. Hernández but had scanned it so quickly I wasn't sure he'd understood it. He'd seemed to think I was some unlucky kid whose name had been put in the gradebook incorrectly due to typographical error or something, so he'd simply scratched out my deadname and written in "LEO" while chuckling about the silly mistakes the people in the office sometimes made.

Which meant he probably thought I was a cis guy, and puberty would soon be working its magic on my body and voice. It was both affirming and depressing at the same time.

But hormones, a voice inside of me whispered. *You could get hormone therapy.*

You haven't even come out to Mom yet, I shot back. *One step at a time, okay?*

I really did like singing, so I enjoyed Choir, and my fellow baritones—of whom there were four—welcomed me with laughing desperation. They were all a grade or two above me, and apparently the year before no one had been able to hear the baritones at all in the winter or spring concerts, so they were thrilled to have one more person added to their ranks. They seemed like good guys, laughing good-naturedly when they hit wrong notes, and the best thing was that they jostled and joked and laughed with me, too, so much so that I really felt like I was one of them despite spending a grand total of forty-five minutes in their company.

By the end of class, they'd started calling me "Leo the Lion" and insisted on us all shouting, "Baritones forever!" and exchanging high fives. Only after this was done was I allowed to go join Robbie, Maya, and Jackson, all of whom looked far too amused by this display.

"They seem nice," Jackson said with an expressive lift of his eyebrows.

My lips twitched, but I fought back the smile. "Shut up."

Jackson laughed, and we headed out of the choir room just as another rowdy chorus of "Baritones forever!" echoed behind us. This time I laughed, too, and as we headed outside—Maya to her bike, Robbie to the bus, and Jackson and me to his car—I realized that this light, golden feeling in my chest was happiness. It probably wouldn't stay long, but it was pretty nice to have it for now.

"Hey, Robbie," Jackson said as Robbie peeled off to wait in line for the bus, "where do you live? If it's not too far, we could give you a lift. I've been driving this guy around for months, so what's one more?"

Robbie gave a cautious smile. "Really? I mean, if you don't mind, I'm over on Elliot Road by the Shaaba Bakery."

That was barely out of our way, so Jackson agreed immediately, and the three of us started for the car with a few final waves to Maya, who was strapping on her purple helmet and tugging her bike out of its slot in the bike rack.

My stomach churned guiltily as we walked away, and I wondered if we should've asked her to come along, too. But after what I'd learned about Maya and Robbie, I wasn't sure trapping them in a car together was the best idea. Besides, the trunk of Jackson's Toyota wasn't exactly built for bike storage, and Maya was a runner, so she probably enjoyed the exercise, right? Sure.

I offered Robbie the front seat, but he waved a hand at me and slid himself into the back. In deference to Robbie's presence, Jackson turned on his music but kept it at a low enough volume that we could all talk to each other and actually hear the responses. It was more politeness than Jackson usually showed to his passengers, but he'd been treating Robbie super nicely all day, and I was glad for it. If anyone deserved kindness, it was Robbie.

We talked about school and other things that didn't matter much, and before I knew it we were turning onto Elliot Road, sailing past the Shaaba Bakery, and pulling into the short driveway Robbie pointed to. Beyond the driveway was a little white house that was freshly painted but looked like a tight fit for more than one person. A smile pulled at Robbie's lips as he looked at it, and I wondered what it must be like to go from a place where you felt hated and shamed to a place where you were unconditionally loved and accepted. No wonder he loved living here.

"Hey, man, thanks for the ride." Robbie exchanged a fist bump with Jackson near my left shoulder, and my arm tingled when Robbie's hand brushed it on the way back. "I really appreciate it. I don't mind taking the bus, but…"

"It's the bus," Jackson finished.

We exchanged "see ya"s, and Jackson and I hung around in the driveway until Robbie had disappeared into the house.

After he had, Jackson threw the Toyota into reverse and shot me a glance. "So, do you like him, or what?"

Alarm tore through me—jeez, was I that obvious?—but I managed an uncaring shrug. "Yeah, he's a nice guy."

"Not what I mean. Do you *like* him?"

Heat flooded my face. "I don't know. I haven't really thought about it."

"Bull crap you haven't. Come on, man. I see the way you look at him. And don't think I missed you groping him in the hallway this morning."

My mind flashed to incident in question, Robbie's body pressed against mine, and suddenly it was very hard to keep my focus on the conversation. "I wasn't groping him. I was hugging him."

"Same thing. Anyway, it's pretty clear he likes you, too, so I guess you guys are gonna run off and get married or something and that'll be great, right?"

He laughed unsteadily, and I shot him a concerned look. And then my brain caught up with what he'd said—*it's pretty clear he likes you, too*—and I momentarily lost the ability to speak. Before I could find my voice again, Jackson cranked up the music and made further conversation impossible. He didn't turn it down until we'd pulled into my driveway, and then he said, without looking at me, "I've gotta get home and run some errands for my mom, but I'll see you at the usual time tomorrow morning, okay?"

I frowned as I grabbed my bookbag. "Uh, yeah, okay. Jackson, are you sure you're—"

"See ya tomorrow!" he said loudly, and the second I closed the car door behind me, he revved the engine and roared off down the road.

Chapter Ten

"Go fish," Maribel said.

"No, *you* go fish," Eleanor retorted.

"It's my turn, and I say *you* go fish."

"I thought we were playing Old Maid," Uncle Shel said helplessly. He looked like a giant sitting next to them on the living room carpet, his legs folded awkwardly and his knee hitting the coffee table every time he moved.

"Uncle Shel, *no*," Maribel and Eleanor said in unison. They dissolved into giggles and started pounding the table and chanting, "No, no, no, no!"

"Uh, Uncle Shel?" I'd been standing in the doorway watching, but I figured I'd let the suffering go on for long enough. "Mom made that list you asked for. Of things that need fixing?"

Shel looked at me like a drowning man might look at a life preserver. "Oh, well, I'd better get started on that right away, then!" He got to his feet with a grunt of effort and narrowly missed hitting his knee on the coffee table again. "Sorry, girls, but you'll have to deal me out this round."

Maribel and Eleanor made sounds of disappointment

but were already grabbing his cards and tucking them into the Go Fish pile. By the time he'd made it to the door and accepted the list I handed him, the twins were back to arguing happily over whose turn it was to go fish.

"Thanks," Shel said under his breath as he scanned the list. "Between you and me, my legs were killing me."

He kindly did not say that Maribel and Eleanor had been driving him up the wall, which I was sure they had been doing, and my respect for Uncle Shel rose another few pegs. I walked with him out into the hallway as he read the list Mom had thrown together.

"Well, nothing here looks too tough. Some rewiring, a broken step, a hole in the drywall, and what's this one at the bottom?"

"Broken pony lamp."

"Ah." He gave the list one more quick scan, then tucked it into his pocket. "Hey, do you want to help me with some of this stuff?"

I stared at him. "Help you?"

"Yeah. I mean, if you want to. I could use an extra hand, and if you're not busy with homework or something…"

"No, I'd love to. I've always wanted to learn how to fix stuff, but—" I broke off, stopping short of saying, *But no one ever thought it was worth teaching me*. Jackson's dad had been enlisting his help in projects around the house for years, but because I'd been read as "girl" for my entire life, no one had ever thought I might want to learn stuff like that. Which would've been messed up even if I weren't a trans guy.

Shel gave me a sympathetic look I figured had something to do with my dad being gone. "Well, hey," he said, his big hand falling into place on my shoulder, "why don't we get started on that broken porch step while there's still light outside, and maybe we'll have time to see about the pony lamp before dinner's ready. Sound good?"

A warm smile pulled at my lips. "Sounds great."

A short time later, I was kneeling beside Shel in the front yard, happily hammering and following his patient instructions. I hit my thumb a few times but got the hang of things pretty quickly, and before I knew it Shel was sitting back with a proud smile on his face.

"And there you go. You've just fixed your first step."

I surveyed my handiwork with a rush of accomplishment. I'd fixed something. Something that had been broken was now unbroken because of me, some nails, and a few swings of my hammer. It was just what I needed after the confusing day I'd had—weird crushes and even weirder best friends—and it might have been a perfect little moment of joy had Aunt Audrey not chosen that exact time to come outside and frown at us.

"What's going on out here?"

She wore a silky green blouse and spotless white jeans with matching heels, and her chin-length dark hair was perfectly in place as usual, her plum-colored lips twisting downward. She and Mom had the same heart-shaped faces and smooth olive skin, but sometimes, looking at Audrey's expression and into her chilly brown eyes, it was hard to imagine she and Mom were even related, let alone sisters.

"Just doing some work around the house," Shel said with a sunny smile that either missed or ignored the disapproval in his wife's tone. "Found myself a great helper, and we've already got the porch steps all fixed up."

"Shel," Audrey said with a lift of one thin eyebrow, "do you really think ___ wants to be crawling around in the dirt nailing boards with you? Despite how she looks, she's a young lady, remember."

Shel looked confused, but I jumped in before he could say anything.

"Aunt Audrey, I want to help him. I like fixing stuff."

She gave that merry little laugh I hated. "Oh, darling, I have no idea why your mother lets you get away with things like this. If you were my daughter—"

"But I'm not," I said, more sharply than I'd intended. Audrey flinched like I'd slapped her. Before she could recover, I turned to Shel. "So, what's next on the list?"

He looked uncertainly from Audrey to me and back again, then pulled the list from his pocket. "Er, hole in the drywall. In the powder room."

"Great, let's get to it."

Audrey didn't say anything as we passed her, but her eyes narrowed dangerously and I felt the weight of her gaze on me as we went. I ignored her, and soon I was crowded in the downstairs powder room with my bear of an uncle and a can of spackle. By the time Mom called us for dinner, we'd taken care of the drywall and started work on Maribel's pony lamp, which mainly just needed a lot of glue and prayers. I stood up feeling like I'd actually accomplished something, and when Shel patted my shoulder and said, "Nice work today, pal," I wondered how it might've felt to have that same moment with my dad.

"You know," Shel told me as we stood side by side in the upstairs bathroom, washing glue and spackle off our hands, "I always kind of wished I could've had a kid to teach things like this to. I love fixing things and building things, and it'd be great to have somebody to share it with. I guess that sounds pretty silly."

"No," I said. "It doesn't. Not at all."

Uncle Shel beamed at me, and after he'd dried his hands, he tossed me the towel and gave me a searching look. "Hey, so is there a name you like to go by, like a nickname or something?"

I went still and glanced at him cautiously. "Why do you ask?"

"I just noticed you make a face every time somebody says your name."

I winced. "Do I?" I hadn't even realized.

"Yeah, but I don't think it's obvious. Just something I noticed."

It occurred to me that someone who had noticed something like that was also probably fully capable of noticing sarcasm in his wife's tone, but perhaps had made a life's study of ignoring it.

There was a moment of silence as I dried my hands and tucked the towel back into its place in the holder.

"Leo," I said quietly.

"Hm?"

"My friends call me Leo."

I wasn't sure what Shel would make of this, but he just smiled and gave an approving nod as if this was exactly what he'd been hoping I would say. As we headed downstairs, he started telling me how he had some extra tools he could give me, and a tool belt he thought would fit me, and this resulted in me having a big grin on my face as I stepped off the landing—and came face to face with Jasmine.

She'd been about to head upstairs, and there was a moment when all I saw in her face was naked surprise and something like panic. And then she slipped past Shel and me without a word and jogged up the stairs. Shel frowned a little but didn't comment, and I thought again about Maya and Robbie, the pain on his face when he looked at her.

"Hey, I'll be right back," I told Uncle Shel. "I forgot there's something I have to tell Jasmine."

He nodded easily and continued on to the dining room, and this left me with no choice but to head back up the stairs and make my way to Jasmine's closed door. I hesitated in front of it for a good count of five, then knocked.

"Come in." She probably figured it was Mom since Mom was the only person in this house who ever bothered to knock.

I pushed open the door and stepped inside.

Jasmine's room was smaller than mine, but she'd somehow managed to make it look open and organized compared to my cramped and messy. There was a tidy desk stacked with school books, a shelf with stuffed animals, books, framed photos, and knick-knacks, and her neatly made bed with its sunny yellow comforter and big white daisy throw pillow. Jasmine sat on the edge of her bed, filing her nails with an emery board.

"I'll be down in just a minute," she said, then glanced up and spotted me standing in her doorway.

She jumped to her feet, lifting her arm like she was about to order me to leave—but then her arm dropped and her shoulders slumped and she said wearily, “At least close the door.”

I pushed the door shut behind me and leaned my back against it. I, as the intruder, was supposed to start the conversation, but I had no idea what to say. I wanted to fix what had gone wrong between us, make her understand that this didn’t have to change anything, but the words stuck in my throat. So I just stood there watching her file her nails, and after she’d finished, she wandered over to her desk and tidied a pile of papers that didn’t need tidying.

“So, why are you here?” she asked. “I’m not going to tell Mom, if that’s what you’re worried about.”

“That’s not why I’m here. I mean, thank you for not telling her, but that’s not why I came up here.”

“Then why?”

The truth found its way out of my mouth at last. “Because I feel like we’re broken, and I want to try to fix us if I can. I just don’t know how. And since you usually know better than me anyway, I thought maybe you’d have an idea.”

Jasmine’s back was to me, her arms folded and posture tense. Her voice was so low it was barely audible. “What makes you think we’re broken?”

“Because you haven’t spoken to me in two days. Because you can’t even look at me.” *Because I’m afraid you hate me for who I am.* “Because I don’t think I explained things very well, and maybe if I had, this would’ve gone differently.”

Jasmine finally turned and looked at me tiredly. “What

is there to explain? You told me already. You're a guy, right? Jackson and your new friends seem totally okay with that, so why shouldn't I be, too?"

"But you're not."

"No." A hint of fire blazed into her eyes. "I'm not. I just don't understand any of this. It's like my big sister is gone and some person I don't even know is standing here instead. I mean, when did this even happen? When did you stop being my sister and become—this?"

The words hurt, but I pushed through it. "Jas, this isn't some big change that happened to me. It's who I've always been. I'm no different than I've been my entire life. I'm still me."

"You're not, though." She stalked over to her bookshelf, snatched up a framed photo that had been lying face-down, and waved it in my face. "Look. Just look. This was back in, what, April? Not even six months ago. You're telling me none of this was real?"

I flinched back but forced myself to look at the photo. It was Jasmine and me sitting together on the back porch swing, our arms intertwined and our heads leaning together as we flashed winning smiles to the camera. My hair was long and carefully styled, soft bangs flopping over my forehead, and I was wearing makeup—foundation, blush, eyeliner, a light coating of lipstick. The developing curves of my body were visible in the snug green shirt and capris I was wearing, and Jasmine and I almost looked like twins with our matching brown hair and similar outfits.

"This is who you used to be." Tears trembled in her

voice and cut through me like knives. "This is my sister, and I want her *back*."

She dropped onto the edge of her bed still holding the frame. Her long hair fell past her shoulders and hid her face from me.

"Look..." My voice came out unsteadily, so I cleared my throat and tried again. "The person in that photo... It's me, but it's a me who's trying to be what everyone else thinks he should be."

She made a strangled noise at the "he" but didn't interrupt.

"All my life, everyone told me I was a girl. They told me I was a girl, and they told me what they meant. Girls do this, girls don't do that. Girls wear this and like this and act like this and I just, I thought that's what I had to do. I thought that's what I had to be. But it never felt right, do you understand? It always felt like I was playing a part, not being who I really was. But now, finally, I've figured it out. I know who I am, and it's the exact same person I've been all along, except now I'm not pretending anymore. Nothing has changed, Jasmine. The only thing that's different is I'm doing what feels right instead of what everyone tells me should feel right. I know it's hard, but I really hope you can understand."

She didn't say anything for a long time. Then she sighed and shook her head. "I can't. And I'm sorry, but I don't think I ever will."

I wanted to cry or shout or throw something, but instead I nodded and left Jasmine's room. I tried to tell myself she would come around eventually like Mr. Raines' father, that she just needed more time to get used to this, but all I felt was loss. Mom was calling from downstairs that dinner was getting cold, though, so I had to put on a non-devastated face and join my family at the table. Jasmine came down shortly thereafter looking normal and cheerful, and we ate our dinner without meeting eyes across the table even once.

After dinner, I retreated to my bedroom under the guise of having homework to do, shut and locked the door, and flopped face-first onto my bed. The flowery comforter Mom had bought me years ago itched against my cheek, so I flipped onto my back and stared around my room. White bookshelves stuffed with dog-eared paperbacks guarded either side of my bed, and notebooks and loose sheets of paper—most filled with scribbled stories, character profiles, and plot outlines—lay in haphazard piles on the desk by the window. Movie posters covered the walls, and at the center of almost every one was a teen guy around my age with cool hair and the kind of confidence I could only dream of.

The latest poster, from some action/fantasy Jasmine and I saw back in April, showed a buff young guy with wavy dark hair and an intense look in his brown eyes. He was from the same part of Mexico as our grandparents, and that plus his general hotness had been enough to convince Jasmine to go with me to what definitely wasn't her usual kind of movie.

I remembered sitting in the dark theater with the popcorn bucket in my lap, Jasmine reaching over from time to time to snag a handful and pop it into her mouth. She was dressed impeccably as usual, a white knitted cardigan draped over a snug olive-green tee and rounded out with her favorite weather-inappropriate capris and a pair of chunky heels. Her makeup was flawless, the blush perfectly blended, the smoky eye expertly applied, and her dark hair spilled over her shoulders in soft, effortless waves.

And I…

I was wearing a similar outfit, but my fingers kept tugging at the fabric of my shirt like it was a size too small, even though it fit just like it was supposed to. Jasmine had styled my hair and done my makeup—she was thinking of starting a makeup and fashion channel online, and she'd claimed she needed someone to practice on. I knew from the mirror that she'd done a perfect job on me, so then why had staring at my reflection felt like locking eyes with a stranger?

A flare of action music from the screen jerked my attention back to the movie, and I was just in time to see the lead actor—Tomás something—race on-screen, his clothes torn and his chiseled face streaked with mud. Beneath the mud, his skin was smoothed bronze, his high cheekbones and square jaw shadowed dramatically by the magic of cinematic lighting. His tattered T-shirt clung to the muscles of his chest in the most flattering way possible, and everything from the set of his broad shoulders to the wide stance of his feet spoke of strength and easy confidence.

My mouth went dry as I looked at him, and a longing I didn't understand curled and twisted in my chest.

Jasmine's elbow nudged my side, her light, floral perfume filling my nose as she leaned in to whisper in my ear. "I can see why you wanted to see this movie. *Damn.*"

I managed a weak smile, and I spent the rest of the film staring at Tomás and trying to untangle what I was feeling. He was insanely good-looking, yeah, but I wasn't looking at him wishing I could kiss him. This was something else, something *more*, and as much as I wanted to know what it was, I was also kind of terrified to examine it too closely.

After the movie, which Jasmine declared was "okay for an action movie, mostly because of the eye candy," we made our usual detour to the mall food court for nachos and then followed the bright red "SALE" signs to one of Jasmine's favorite clothing stores. She spotted four different outfits she wanted to try on almost immediately, leaving me wandering the aisles on my own. Caught up in thoughts of Tomás' perfect pecs—which we'd seen on full display for the entire last sequence of the movie, because of course—I drifted toward the back of the store. Between one absentminded step and the next, I found myself in the guys' section.

My first instinct was to turn around and head back to the girls' area, slide my fingers over the racks of baby doll tees, impractically thin sweaters, and flirty skirts. But instead, my steps drew me deeper into a forest of muted colors, sturdy flannels, and pants with deep pockets. I gazed up at mannequins with broad, flat chests and posters of happy young guys in jackets, T-shirts, and bootcut jeans. The longing Tomás had ignited in me grew and grew, until finally I couldn't take it anymore and grabbed a random shirt, jacket, and pair of jeans from the racks and fled to the dressing room.

I peeled off my snug top and stretchy jeans and slid my

body into thicker, more durable fabric. The jeans felt stiff but good, the legs a little long but not ridiculously so, and the shirt and jacket were cool and weighty against my skin. I stood taller, widening my stance and lifting my chin like an action hero posing on a cliffside while the wind blew heroically through his hair, and it felt *good.* It felt right.

And then I faced the mirror, and all the good feelings trickled away.

The clothes were right, but they looked wrong on me. The rise of my chest under the T-shirt was wrong, the swell of my hips was wrong, the hair and the makeup and just all of it—it was all wrong. I wasn't supposed to look like this, and I'd never noticed until this very moment, wearing clothes that felt so right but looked *so wrong*.

A knock on the dressing room door made me jump, and my chest tightened as Jasmine's voice sang through the thin, slatted wood. "I know you're in there—I recognize your socks! What are you trying on?"

Panic tore through me, but the door was already opening—how had I forgotten to lock it?—and then the harsh fluorescents flooded in to give Jasmine a spotlight view of what I was wearing.

Her perfectly shaped brows lifted in surprise, and then her lips quirked and she burst out laughing. "Oh, my God. What is this, Halloween? Why are you wearing that?"

Mortification pooled in my gut, and I tried to tug off the jacket but got my arm stuck in it halfway. "I just…I don't know. I wanted to try something different."

Jasmine laughed again and slid her arm around my shoulders. "Well, it's definitely *different*. Look, you're my sister and I love you, and that's why I have to tell you the truth. I hope you'd do the same thing for me if I ever..." Her gaze roved up and down my outfit again and she shook her head. "But, yeah, this look? Really not working for you."

I swallowed a sudden lump in my throat and managed a weak laugh. "No?"

"Absolutely not. It's just not right for your body type, you know? Here, hang on a sec." She ducked out of the room and came back with a long-sleeved crop-top and a pair of figure-hugging black jeans. "This is more what you should be wearing. Way more flattering. Way more *you*."

I took the clothes with numb fingers and forced a crooked smile. "Yeah, I guess you're right."

She beamed and patted my shoulder excitedly. "Hey, you should be the first guest on my channel! We can show you wearing, like, completely the *wrong* clothes, like this, and then I can style you into something that fits you better, like this. What do you think?"

"Um. Yeah. Sure." The words felt like ash on my tongue.

Jasmine skipped off after that, content in a fashion disaster averted, and I was left alone in the changing room with a sick, helpless feeling in my stomach. I carefully removed the jacket, shirt, and jeans and returned them to their hangers. My regular clothes felt too snug and restraining as I pulled them on, and I hated the way they outlined the curves of my body. I'd always hated that, I realized, and I had to sit down hard on the bench seat as a thousand little signs piled on top of each other and buried me underneath.

That night after dinner, I locked myself in my room with my laptop and, with shaking fingers, typed "transgender" into the internet search bar. The daylight faded around me until the glaring white of the computer screen was the only illumination, but I kept reading, and I eventually fell down a rabbit hole of videos with titles like "How I realized I was trans" and "All about my transition (FTM)." It was nearly eleven o'clock when I finally snapped the laptop shut and sank back against my pillows, my heart racing like I'd just run a marathon.

It probably wasn't true. I was probably just overreacting, or jumping to conclusions, or… Something. *Something*. But then why had I teared up watching a guy a few years older than me talk about going shopping with his mom for new clothes? Why had the sight of him with his facial hair and low voice and flat chest made the little spark of longing in my chest flare into a full-on bonfire of *oh my God, I want that*?

The next day, I dug around in the back of my closet and finally pulled out an old sweatshirt of my dad's I'd rescued from the thrift store pile after the funeral. It was gray-green and soft with wear, the letters in "Pittsburgh" so faded they were hardly readable anymore. It smelled like the back of my closet, but I breathed in deeply as I pulled it on over my head.

It was a little big on me but not as big as I'd expected, and as I stood in front of the mirror, no makeup and my hair tied back, the smile that came to lips was warm and real. And if Jasmine gave me a weird look at breakfast and made a pointed comment asking if I was "really going to wear that," it didn't dim the sense of rightness that had finally settled over me. I wasn't quite ready to make the leap to labeling myself, but this was a step, and it was one I finally felt ready to take.

It was another month before I felt ready to cut my hair, and a month after that before Jasmine finally gave me up as a lost cause and stopped asking to do my clothes and makeup for her channel. She enlisted the help of some of her friends at school instead, and as she spent more time with them and on her own fashion projects, I spent more time either hanging out with Jackson or holed up in my room, writing or doing trans-related research.

Occasionally I would look at Jasmine across the dinner table and think about telling her—explaining everything I was feeling and why I couldn't be her perfect almost-twin anymore. But every time I considered it, my mind flashed back to her laughter in the changing room, the almost pitying look she sometimes shot at me when I emerged from my bedroom wearing comfortable sweatshirts, jeans, and sneakers and not a drop of makeup. And I couldn't do it. I couldn't tell her.

And now she knew, and it was worse than I'd ever imagined.

I'd had to push her away to find myself, but I'd always figured she would still be there when I was ready to come back. But now it was looking like the cost of finding myself was losing my sister, and what if I never got her back?

Chapter Eleven

"Hey, Dad," I said as the dreamscape froze around me.

"Hi." Dad looked around approvingly. "Did you do this?"

We were in the school gym, and after a lot of failed attempts, I'd managed to conjure up a hot tub like the one Dad's sister Dana had at her house when I was a kid. It was big enough for five or six people, and before Dad's appearance froze everything, the jets had been bubbling nicely against my back and legs. It turned out that when what I was dreaming up wasn't connected to my innate sense of self-worth, it was a heck of a lot easier to manifest.

"Nice work," Dad said.

I was proud of the hot tub, and I felt like my handyman activities with Uncle Shel had given me the confidence I'd needed to create it. But what really made me feel good was what I'd done to myself. I sat in the hot tub in swim trunks and nothing else, and my chest was flat and smooth and male, no binder necessary.

"So." Dad strolled closer to me with his hands in his jean pockets. "Think you're ready to do some dream walking?"

"I think I've mastered walking, thanks."

Dad shot me a wry look and snapped his fingers, and suddenly the hot tub was gone and I stood next to him in the clothes I'd worn to school that day. My hands immediately went to my chest, and I was relieved to find it flat and binder-less.

"So, here's the thing," Dad said. "We're all connected. The people in your life, the people you care about and who care about you—even the people you can't stand. They're all joined to you, and that makes it possible to find them in the dreamscape and walk into their dreams."

I frowned. "Find them where? How?"

Dad nodded at something ahead of us, and I blinked. We were no longer in my dream version of the school gym. We stood in a bluish space lined with doors that stretched off into infinity in either direction. I shivered at the sight, anxiety forming a heavy lump in my throat.

"Easy." Dad's hand was warm and reassuring on my shoulder. "I know it looks daunting, but it's actually pretty simple. All you do is close your eyes and think about the person whose dreams you want to visit, and the right door will appear. Try it."

My brow creased. It couldn't actually be that easy, could it? Dad watched me with a faint, encouraging smile, waiting, so I released a soft exhale and closed my eyes. I figured I should think of Mom or Jackson or someone I knew really well, but as it had been doing all day, Robbie's face flashed in front of my eyes when I tried to focus. A whisper of wind brushed my face and Dad's fingers on my shoulder gave a little squeeze.

"There. See? I knew you could do it."

I opened my eyes. The endless line of doors had disappeared. Now there was only one door, a plain white one like I'd seen Robbie vanish into earlier that day.

"You want me to go in with you?" Dad asked.

My stomach twisted as I glanced at him. "I don't know. Is it dangerous? Could I get stuck in there or something?"

Dad breathed out a laugh as he shook his head. "No, it's just like any other dream, except it isn't yours. Nothing in it can hurt you, and you can wake up any time, or go back to your own dreams by picturing a door to lead you back." He nodded at the door in front of us. "Just make sure you knock first before you go in."

"Why do I knock?"

"To let the dreamer decide if they want to let you in or not. We only go where we're wanted, Leo. If someone doesn't want you in their dreams, they have a right to keep you out." He patted my shoulder again and took a small step back. "You're gonna do great."

He was fading again, and urgency filled my chest. "Dad, how did you learn to do this?"

"My dad taught me." He was nearly gone, and his voice echoed to me as if from a great distance. "And his mother taught him. It's passed down from father to son, or mother to daughter, or parent to child. From dreamer to dreamer…"

He was gone before his words finished echoing in my dream ears. I stood feeling alone in the blueness of the dreamscape, and then I stepped up to the door to Robbie's dreams.

• • •

As I considered the closed white door, it occurred to me again that most likely none of this was real. Much as I wanted to believe my dad actually had returned from the grave to give me dreaming lessons, it was way more likely this was just a particularly weird, vivid dream of mine. But as long as I was in it, I might as well keep going, right?

Remembering Dad's advice, I knocked on the door first—three times, lightly—and waited to see if anything would happen. There was a pause, as if the person on the other side of the door was considering me, and then a lock clicked and the door swung inward. I drew a deep breath and entered.

I stood in a grassy expanse dotted with trees. Sun shone down from a cloudless sky, and laughter and voices echoed from somewhere up ahead. The air smelled fresh and sweet, and it was warm but not too warm, perfect for being outside. When I followed the voices, I came into view of a family crowded together on a picnic sheet on the grass. There was a mother, a father, and two young children, and they were laughing and talking and eating and just seeming to enjoy the day. It wasn't until I got closer that I saw one of the kids was fair-skinned and brown-eyed with a mop of reddish-blond hair, while the other was slimmer and darker, with thick black hair down to her shoulders.

"This is my favorite memory," a soft voice said beside me.

It was Robbie. Teenage Robbie, the Robbie I knew, the one I'd been staring at practically all day. He was close enough to touch, wearing a soft red T-shirt and gray sweatpants, his hair a messy mop and his lips bent in a faint smile.

"Maya had been with us for a few months, and it was the first time we really felt like a family. Mom and Dad were happy, Maya was happy, I was happy. We didn't know any better back then."

Robbie's dad threw a piece of popcorn into the air and caught it in his mouth, then tossed another piece toward little Robbie, who had his mouth open and waiting. It hit Robbie square in the forehead, bounced off, and hit the side of Maya's face, and the whole family burst out laughing.

Except… I rubbed my eyes and blinked a few times, but no matter how I squinted, I couldn't make out any distinguishing features of Robbie's mom or dad. Maya and Robbie were crystal clear, from their bright, childlike eyes to their summery T-shirts and shorts, but their parents were less substantial, just mother- and father-shaped figures doing mother- and father-shaped things. I slipped away from teenage Robbie and drew closer, but when I stood facing Robbie's parents from the edge of the picnic sheet, inches away from the laughing kids, I still couldn't make out their faces. It was like I was seeing them from far away despite how close I stood to them, and I glanced back at Robbie with a frown—but he wasn't there anymore.

The dream shifted with a lurch, and I was somewhere else. A school hallway, painted in unfamiliar colors. Robbie's old school? A younger version of Robbie was walking down the hall, head bent to the floor and textbooks clutched protectively to his chest. Some faceless figures walked toward him, and one of their shoulders collided hard with his as they passed. Robbie stumbled backward and crashed into the locker next to him, and a low, laughing voice said, "Watch where you're going, freak."

The dream shifted again, and glimpses of other scenes flashed by almost too quickly to take them in—Robbie drawing furiously in his notebook while mocking voices surrounded him; Robbie staring at his reflection in a bathroom mirror, a pair of scissors held to his shoulder-length curls with shaking fingers; Robbie flinching as a deep male voice boomed in his ears; sadness and betrayal blooming on his face as Maya fled up a flight of stairs and a door slammed behind her.

And then the dream gave one last dizzying jerk, and I breathed in the warm, familiar scents of pencil dust, dry erase markers, and floor wax. I was in a dim, quiet classroom, and Robbie stood nearby studying me curiously.

"I'm usually alone in those dreams." His soft voice seemed to come from all directions at once. "What are you doing here, Leo?"

It couldn't be real, but I felt flustered even so, like I'd been caught at something I shouldn't be doing. "I, um. Sorry. My dad told me to come through the door. I tried to think of someone else, but I kept thinking about you, and it led me here. I knocked and you let me in."

Robbie stepped closer. I was frozen to the spot and couldn't move, even when he took another step forward so we stood nearly nose to nose, close enough that I could see myself reflected in the brown of his eyes. I knew I should move, envision a door back to my own dream and get out of there, but my body was locked in place.

Robbie lifted a hand and, very gently, pressed his palm to the side of my face. "You feel real," he said quietly.

His hand was as warm and solid as it had been earlier in the hallway, and I leaned my cheek into his touch, my spinning thoughts going blissfully still.

"Are you?" he whispered, his breath a soft puff on my lips. His thumb stroked my cheek, and then his hand slid back into my hair and I thought he might be about to kiss me. I wanted that to happen but didn't want it to happen like this, in a dream that may or may not have even been real, so I leapt backward and stammered out, "I-I have to go."

When I turned to run, the door back to my own dreams was there. I dashed through it without a backward glance, and it slammed behind me the second I was through.

Chapter Twelve

The next morning I stood at my closet, staring at the sequined blue dress Mom had bought for me for my birthday. It was modestly cut and looked like it would fit perfectly, and I knew Mom had taken great care to find it. The brand name on the label told me it had been expensive, and while I probably should have just been grateful she'd cared enough to get it for me, all I felt was dread. The thought of putting it on made me feel physically ill, and I knew I would never be able to wear it, not even for one night, not even for my mom.

I pulled it carefully from the closet and, before I could lose my nerve, took it on a walk over to my mom's closed bedroom door. It was still early enough that no one was up and about yet, but I'd heard the shower go on and then off in Mom's room and knew she was awake.

I knocked quietly, ignoring the muffled giggles coming from Eleanor and Maribel's room next door.

"Come in," Mom said.

I went in.

Mom was at her vanity in her favorite soft white bathrobe, her wet dark hair wrapped up in a towel as she dabbed concealer under her eyes. An array of makeup bottles and little wands and brushes lay in neat rows in front of her, and I marveled that even this small part of her morning routine was so orderly.

She flashed me a smile through the mirror. "Well, you're up early. What's on your mind?" Her gaze flickered from my face to the dress, and she turned around in her chair. "Oh, no, does it not fit?"

"Um, in a manner of speaking." I pushed the door closed behind me and rested my back against it. "Look, I really appreciate you buying me this dress. I know it was expensive, and I know you thought I'd look good in it, and maybe I would, but…I can't wear it."

Mom gave me a kind smile. "Sweetheart, if it doesn't fit, we can have it altered. Or if it's the style that's the problem, we can exchange it for one you like better. I shouldn't have bought it without you there to approve it, anyway, so that's my fault. Look, we can go on Saturday before your birthday, have a girls' day out or something. We can get your lip waxed, too, and—"

"Mom, *no*." She blinked, brows lifting and lips forming a question, but I had the momentum finally and forced the words out. "It's not that I don't want to wear this dress, I don't want to wear any dress. And I don't want to have my lip waxed, either."

Mom studied me with her head tilted to the side, and there was no anger or judgment in her eyes, just confusion. "Well, of course, sweetheart, if that's what you want. What do you want to wear instead?"

I swallowed. I thought about Dad saying, *It's not them you have to believe in. It's yourself.*

"A suit," I said.

Mom nodded slowly. "Okay. That could work, too. We'll exchange the dress and get you a nice pants suit."

"Not a pants suit. A guy's suit. Like a guy would wear."

My hands were shaking, and my heartbeat pulsed faster in my throat. I tried some of Robbie's 4-7-8 breathing and felt a little steadier.

"Oh." A faint line of confusion creased Mom's brow, but she shrugged. "Sure, if that's what you want."

And that was it. Mom had said I could wear a suit, a *guy's* suit, to my birthday party.

Relief flooded through me and I nearly sank back against the door. "Really? Thank you. I'd really like that."

Mom beamed back at me. "Then that's what we'll do." She got to her feet and came to stand next to me, smelling like strawberry body wash and the strong astringent lotion she used on her face every morning. "Look, sweetheart, I know you have your own style, and I want you to be able to express yourself however you want. If this is how you want to do it, then that's completely fine with me. Just… I hope you know that you don't have to be ashamed of your body."

My relief was buried under an avalanche of discomfort and embarrassment, and I made a face.

"I'm serious," she said. "Everyone your age feels this way at some point. Your body is changing, and it can be strange and a little frightening. But I promise you, you'll get used to it. And before you know it, you'll feel confident enough to want to show it off. It's you, it's your body, and there's nothing wrong with it no matter how you might feel now, okay? Your feelings *will* change."

The words cut right to the secret heart of me and stabbed. "I better go get ready for school," I mumbled.

As I fled the room, leaving the dress behind on Mom's bed, she called something after me about maybe going suit shopping on Saturday, but I barely heard her. I ran to my bedroom and closed the door, then leaned against it with my eyes closed, breathing hard.

Your feelings will change. It's your body and there's nothing wrong with it.

I'd thought I was past this, but the doubt came surging up around me again, poking holes in my certainty and deflating the confidence I'd been painstakingly building. What if I did get past this? What if I got a little older and suddenly didn't feel trans anymore? What if after coming out and asking everyone to call me by a different name and get used to seeing me as a guy, I had to turn around and say *never mind!* and ask them to go back to seeing me as a girl? What if I started taking hormones and got surgery and then realized I wasn't a guy after all?

I lived in the fear and doubt and panic for a long, horrible moment, but instead of spiraling out of control, I forced myself to focus on my breathing, to ground myself like Robbie had said. My bare feet pressing into the carpet. The little ache in my neck from where I'd slept on it wrong. The softness of my night shirt against my palms. Breathe in, hold, breathe out.

When I felt a little steadier, I grabbed my phone from the nightstand and pulled up a number I'd only recently put in. As the line rang with a tinny buzz in my ear, I caught sight of the time on my alarm clock—5:42 AM—and almost hung up. I didn't, though. I clutched the phone to my ear and waited.

After another few rings, there was a click and Robbie's drowsy voice in my ear. "H'llo?"

I swallowed and tried not to think of his hand on my cheek, his fingers sliding through my hair. "Hey."

There was a clatter and some rustling, and his voice came back sounding more awake. "Hey. Leo. Are you okay?"

"I'm sorry to call so early—"

"Don't worry about it. I should be up by now, anyway. What's going on?"

I sat down on my bed and closed my eyes, telling myself firmly that I would not cry, I would not cry. "Um, I guess I was just wondering. How do you know you're not pretending?"

There was a short silence. "What do you mean?"

"About being trans." I pressed a hand to my face and wished I hadn't called, but there was nowhere to go now but forward. "How do you know you're really trans and you won't change your mind about it someday or something?"

Another silence, and I was afraid he was offended or would go the opposite way and laugh at me for being ridiculous. Instead, he took a breath and let it out slowly.

"I guess I don't know," he said. "How can anybody know how they'll feel in the future, about anything? All I know is how I feel now, and how I've felt for my entire life. And if something does change someday, I guess I'll just have to deal with it. But I don't think it's going to change for me, and I don't think it'll change for you, either."

"It's like I'm unmaking my whole life." My voice trembled dangerously near tears but thankfully didn't cross over. "I'm asking people to change everything they've ever known about me, and what if I'm wrong? What if I go through all this and then in two years or something I just suddenly stop feeling this way and want to go back to how it was before?"

"Did you tell your mom?" Robbie asked quietly. "Is that where this is coming from?"

"No. I mean, not exactly. I told her I didn't want to wear a dress to my birthday, I wanted to wear a suit instead, and she gave me this talk about how it's totally normal not to like your body, and someday I'll feel differently, and I don't know. It just really got to me."

"Of course it did. She's your mom." Robbie let out a breath that hissed over the receiver. "Look, don't think about what she said, think about how you feel, deep down. Try to picture yourself in the future, living your life, going to college or doing whatever you want to do. What do you see when you picture that future you?"

I thought again about the me I'd been in my dreams, relaxed and proud in the hot tub with my flat, bare chest visible over the bubbling water. I tried to envision some future version of myself in Mom's pencil skirts and blouses and heels, or her Hillary Clinton style pants suits or the snug black workout gear she wore to the gym, but it all just felt wrong. It wasn't me. I even thought about myself dressing like Ms. Yamaguchi, wearing what were essentially guys' clothes and keeping my hair short but still living as a woman, being called *she* and *her* or even *they*, but it didn't work. When I thought about who was at the very heart of me, I didn't see a girl or woman, even a cool, tough one like Mom or Ms. Yamaguchi.

"I see a guy," I said.

"Then that's who you are," Robbie said. The simplicity of it cut through my panic and made me breathe a relieved sigh.

"God, Robbie, I'm sorry. You shouldn't have to keep dealing with stuff like this."

"Stuff like what?"

"Me in a panic."

"Hey, I've been there. I still go there sometimes. Being able to help you is the only good thing that's ever come out of my anxiety, so I figure it's worth it just for that."

I felt warm all over, and a smile spread over my face as I imagined Robbie wrapped up in blankets in a bedroom I'd never seen, his curls tousled and his eyes sleepy.

"I guess I better let you go," I said.

"Yeah, I should probably put on some clothes before I try to go to school."

I grinned. "See you later."

"See you. And Leo?"

"Yeah?"

"You got this."

I thanked him and hung up, and I lay on my bed grinning stupidly at the ceiling for a good two or three minutes before I remembered I should probably get up and get ready for school.

Robbie was right. I could do this.

Chapter Thirteen

I was a little worried things might be weird between Jackson and me after whatever had been going on with him the day before, but he gave the usual wry smile from under his sunglasses as I slid into the passenger seat.

"What up, dude?" he said.

"Oh, you know. Existential angst, family drama, the usual." I eyed him carefully. "How are you doing?"

"No complaints, my man. No complaints." He slid the Toyota into gear and got us underway. "We're making a little detour today, by the way."

"Oh, yeah?"

"Yeah, I thought we'd pick up your favorite guy over on Elliot and save him from having to take the bus." He shot me a sideways glance. "I heard some guys from his old school were picking on him on the bus the other day."

I straightened in my seat, a sudden, protective burst of anger roaring in my chest. "What? Who? What were they saying?"

Jackson raised a *calm down* hand at me. "I don't know exactly, but you know how crappy people can be sometimes.

Anyway, I figured we have space in the backseat, so why not?"

"Thank you," I said fervently. "Really."

Jackson's eyes flickered toward mine with an emotion I didn't understand, and then he fixed his gaze firmly on the road ahead. "You can sit in the back with him if you want. You know, spend some quality time."

My pulse betrayed me by speeding up at the thought of Robbie and me sitting inches apart in the cozy privacy of the back seat, but I ignored it and threw Jackson a frown. "Why would I sit in the back with him?"

"I don't know, I just figured you'd probably want to, like, hold hands or make out or something. Whatever people do."

"Jackson, Robbie and I aren't together."

"Maybe not yet. But that's where this is going, isn't it? I mean, I'm not stupid."

"I'm not so sure about that," I said. "What's going on with you?"

"What? I'm trying to be supportive."

"You are being supportive, but, like, *too* supportive. And weird. Come on, seriously, what's going on?"

To my surprise, he pulled us over to the side of the road and flipped on the parking brake. We sat in silence for a few seconds, and I realized he hadn't even tried to put on his music this morning. Was he sick? Something had to be seriously wrong.

He didn't look at me as he spoke. "Look, I just…I can see that you like him, and I don't want to stand in your way. Even if it means…"

"What?"

He sighed and took off his sunglasses so he could pinch the bridge of his nose between his fingers. "Even if it means we don't get to hang out so much anymore."

Relief poured through me, and I couldn't help laughing. "Oh my God, is that what this is about? You think I'm gonna stop hanging out with you to spend time with Robbie now?"

He threw me a dark glance as he slipped the sunglasses into his jacket pocket. "Well, yeah."

"Dude, I'm touched that you care, but that's not gonna happen. I don't know what's going to happen with Robbie—I mean, probably nothing. I doubt he thinks of me as anything more than a fellow anxious trans friend. But even if we got together tomorrow, it wouldn't change anything with you and me. You're my best friend, and that's not going to change."

Jackson directed his next comments to the floor mats, his voice barely above a mumble. "It's just that it's always been you and me, and then suddenly this year there's Robbie, and Maya, and that Otis guy from gym, and those guys in Choir, and I guess I just feel like you don't need me so much anymore."

"Psht," I said eloquently. I unbuckled my seatbelt so I could slide over and wrap my arms around Jackson in an awkward sideways car hug. "I will always need you," I murmured into his shoulder. "I mean, who else can I count on to untangle me from my binder and not even laugh when he does it?"

When I pulled back, Jackson was grinning at me, and I

gave him a quick grin in return before I slid back into my seat.

We got underway again, and we'd gone a mile or so down the road when Jackson said, almost grudgingly, "I'm pretty sure he does like you, though."

The words sent a thrill through me, but I beat it back with the all-powerful stick of self-deprecation and denial. "I really doubt it. I mean, I think he likes me, but I don't think he *likes* me. Why would he? We just met, and I've already had two full-on anxiety attacks in front of him. That's not exactly the road to romance."

Jackson rolled his eyes. "Dude, come on, it's so obvious. The way he looks at you, and the way he is when you're around… He's totally into you."

"I shall agree to disagree," I said. But his words still settled into a quiet, secret place in my brain and made a tiny seed of hope sprout there.

Robbie was waiting on the porch of his aunt's little white house when we got there, and because I had a serious problem, the mere sight of him in his cozy maroon hoody and jeans made my heart give a little leap in my chest.

Just as we pulled up and Robbie got to his feet, the door behind him opened and a woman with short dark hair bustled outside and handed him what I assumed to be a bagged lunch. He laughed and took it, and she gave him a squeezing hug that danced him back and forth before releasing him. She stayed on the porch watching as Robbie jogged down to the car, and when she waved at Jackson and me, we smiled and waved back.

Robbie was still grinning as he climbed into the

backseat, bringing with him a flood of clean scent—soap and pine and fresh air. "My aunt," he said, hefting the brown paper bag, "doesn't seem to think too highly of the cafeteria food. To be honest, neither do I."

We all gave her one last wave as we pulled away, and I watched through the side mirror as she retreated back into the house and closed the door.

"She seems nice," I said.

Robbie's voice was warm. "She's the best."

"All right, boys," Jackson said, "prepare yourselves. I've got some new tunes that just dropped this morning, and we may be the first people on this continent to listen to them. Are you ready?"

"Probably not," I said.

"Sure," Robbie said gamely from the back seat, though I could tell he was bracing himself.

"All right," Jackson said. "Hold onto your skulls, because this is gonna blow. Your. Minds."

The song that blasted over the speakers sounded pretty much identical to all the other ones Jackson liked listening to, but he nodded passionately along to it like it was a revelation, and every now and then he'd stare over at me after a guitar riff like he couldn't believe what he'd just heard. Through the rearview mirror, I saw Robbie grinning and shaking his head, and when our eyes met, we both had to look away or we might have burst out laughing.

The song lasted the full eight minutes it took us to drive to school, and by the time we got there, my ears were ringing, Robbie was leaning wearily back against the seat cushions, and Jackson was shaking his head with a look of musical nirvana on his face.

"That," he said as he switched off the car, "was amazing. Thanks for sharing that with me, my dudes."

"Sure thing," I said, and Robbie and I shared another grin as we climbed out of the car.

We'd only taken a few steps when Robbie's phone buzzed. He dug it out of his pocket, his brow furrowing. "It's my aunt. Hello?"

There was a rush of tense-sounding words on the other end, and Robbie's face went pale. "What? Is she okay?"

More tense talking. "Yeah, of course. I mean, I can take the bus. No, you go straight there. I'll get there as soon as I can."

He hung up the phone looking shaken, and Jackson and I stood silently watching, waiting for the bomb to drop.

Finally, Robbie met our eyes. "Maya's in the hospital. I guess she was biking to school this morning and somebody hit her."

The bottom dropped out of my stomach. "Somebody *hit* her? Like with their car?"

"Yeah. Side-swiped her and knocked her off her bike. They think she's gonna be okay, but they're still checking her out, so they don't know for sure yet. My aunt's going straight there to be with my mom, so I'm gonna go grab a bus and try and get there—"

"Whoa, whoa, whoa." Jackson took hold of Robbie's arm before he could wander more than a few steps in the direction of the road and the city bus stop. "Don't be stupid. We'll drive you."

Robbie looked between us and shook his head. "I couldn't ask you to do that."

"You're not asking," I said. "We're offering."

"But school—"

"Forget about school," Jackson said. "Come on, or we're leaving without you."

We headed back to the car, and after a quick deliberation, I climbed into the back with Robbie and buckled myself into the seat next to him. Robbie gave me a surprised look that settled into gratitude, and as Jackson got us underway, I reached across the seat and took Robbie's hand. I'd just planned to hold it for a second, maybe give it an encouraging squeeze, but his fingers wrapped snugly around mine and we held hands the whole way to the hospital.

Robbie led the way into the waiting room, his gaze scanning back and forth in search of his aunt. I scanned the room, too, and didn't see her—but I definitely noticed when Robbie came to a dead stop in front of me, his gaze fixed on a woman with curly reddish-blond hair sitting by herself near the nurse's station. His mom? I wondered if he would even want to talk to her, though he had to have known that he would see her if he came here.

I jerked my thumb in the direction of the door and the car we'd left parked a few rows down. "Hey, do you want us to…?"

"No." The word shot from Robbie's lips without

hesitation. "No, stay." He took a deep breath and walked over to his mom.

She didn't notice him at first, her gazed fixed on the far doorway as if waiting for someone to come through it with news. Unlike the blurred dream vision I'd had of her, her features came into focus when we got closer—a pale, rounded face, freckles, and light blue eyes. She was chewing on her lower lip, her brow furrowed in worry. When she turned her head and found someone standing next to her, she leapt to her feet with her mouth open as if ready to ask if there had been any updates on Maya's condition, then froze when she saw who was standing there.

A name that was definitely not "Robbie" fell from her lips, and I winced.

"Robbie," he corrected gently.

She didn't argue but also didn't correct herself, and silence fell between them. There was a moment when I thought neither of them were going to speak or move for the rest of their lives, and then Robbie's mom sniffled and said, "Come here," and folded him into a hug.

He fell into her arms and they hugged each other tightly. Robbie was only a few inches taller than his mother, still able to rest his head on her shoulder as he hugged her. When they pulled back, Robbie wiped his eyes and cleared his throat before he spoke.

"How is she?"

Mrs. Welsh glanced at the empty doorway again and shook her head. "They haven't been telling me much, but the nurse said they were optimistic. They don't think she has a concussion, but she did hit her head, and they wanted to do some tests to make sure everything is okay. I just wish your father was here. He always seems to know what to do."

Robbie's expression darkened, but all he said was, "Did Aunt Allie not get here yet?"

"Oh, she went to get some coffee." Mrs. Welsh waved vaguely in the direction of some unseen hospital cafeteria. "I told her I'd rather have tea, but she said coffee is what people always drink on TV when they're waiting in hospitals, so that's what we should have. I think she was joking. I'm never really sure."

Robbie smiled a little at that, and then at last he seemed to remember that Jackson and I were standing awkwardly a few feet away, listening but trying not to intrude.

"Oh, Mom, these are two of my friends from school." He gestured to us, and we drew a few steps closer. "This is Jackson, and this is Leo. They drove me here so I wouldn't have to take the bus."

"That was very kind of you," Mrs. Welsh said. There was a coolness to her voice, and her gaze lingered on me for a second longer than it did on Jackson, going from my face to my chest and back again before moving back to Robbie. "___ and her sister have always been close, so I'm sure she appreciates you bringing her here."

Robbie flinched at the blatant misgendering and deadnaming, his shoulders pulling inward and his gaze dropping. I waited for him to correct her, but he just stared down at his shoes and said nothing.

"Well, I guess we'd better get comfortable," his mother said, apparently having missed the mental devastation she'd just caused her son. "Are your friends staying, or do they have to get back to school?"

"We're staying," I said, because it was clearer to me than ever that Robbie needed us here. "Maya's our friend, too."

"Yeah," Jackson said firmly. "We're all friends here." He patted Robbie companionably on the back. "Anyway, we're this guy's ride, and no way are we leaving him stranded here."

Jackson hit particularly hard on the words *guy* and *him*, which made Robbie's mother look at him coldly. It was worth it, though, because Robbie stood a bit taller, a small smile tugging at his mouth.

Robbie's mother returned to her seat without further comment, and we joined her, Robbie next to his mom, me next to Robbie, Jackson on the end to my right. A small TV perched over the nurses' station was showing some soap opera about attractive rich white people being attractive, rich, and white, and the nurses were busily filling out forms, talking to patients and loved ones, and jogging up and down the hall holding clipboards.

Everywhere was the cool, antiseptic smell of the hospital, and it was hard not to think about the last time I'd been here, waiting for news on Dad after he'd collapsed on the racquetball court. I'd been sure he'd be okay, because he was Dad and it would've been impossible for him not to be okay. I hadn't realized my entire life was about to change, but at least I'd been able to enjoy those last few moments of innocence before it had.

Realizing my thoughts were wandering in a dark

direction, I glanced over at Jackson to see how he was handling our new hospital waiting room-based reality. To my surprise, he was staring intently at the TV, his eyes wide as White Blond Woman Number 1 told White Blond Woman Number 2, "He's not your husband. He was *never* your husband."

"Are you seriously watching this?" I murmured.

Jackson glanced at me guiltily, then shrugged and turned his gaze back to the TV. "My mom loves this stuff. Must be genetic."

I shook my head and glanced at Robbie, who was studying his fingers as they tapped together in his lap. Beyond him, his mother was doing the exact same thing, and for a moment even their faces synched up in the same worried, brow-furrowing expression. Then a doctor came striding briskly out through the far doorway, and Mrs. Welsh jumped to her feet and hurried to meet her.

The rest of us got to our feet more slowly and followed, and we were just in time to hear the doctor say, "—no internal damage or signs of concussion that we can see, so she should be fine. We'll keep her here for observation just to make sure there's nothing else we haven't detected, but after that she'll be free to go home."

"No broken bones?" Mrs. Welsh asked worriedly. "No sprains or strains or—"

"Just some bruises and scrapes, nothing to worry about." The doctor had a low, calming voice, straight dark hair pulled into a tidy ponytail, and a name tag that identified her as Dr. Claire Wu. "She's very lucky. The car only grazed her, but if she hadn't been wearing her helmet, we'd probably be having a very different conversation right now. I'd encourage her to be more careful about where she rides in the future. Back streets are best, but even those aren't a guarantee of safety. Cyclists die every day, you know."

"Oh, I know." Mrs. Welsh's eyes were wide. "We keep telling her riding that bike around is dangerous, but you know kids. They never want to listen to their parents. Can I see her?"

Dr. Wu hesitated. "We're still running some tests, but I suppose it wouldn't hurt for you to be in the room while we do them. Just you, though, I'm afraid," she added with an apologetic glance at Robbie, Jackson, and me. "The rest of you can come in when we've finished."

"Yes, of course," Mrs. Welsh said. She followed the doctor without even a backward glance at Robbie.

Robbie's shoulders sank as his mom disappeared down the hallway, and while I wanted to comfort him, I wasn't sure what I could say to make this any better. It was clear his mom cared about him, but it was a careful, distant sort of care, one that was easily overshadowed by the clear and less conditional love she seemed to have for Maya.

Jackson slung a supportive arm over Robbie's shoulders. "Well, I guess we wait, then. You guys want me to explain what's happening on this show so you can watch? It's pretty interesting, actually…"

We were spared listening to Jackson's soap opera summary because Robbie's aunt returned to the waiting room at that very moment, holding two insulated paper cups and moving with the same boundless energy she'd displayed on the porch earlier. When she caught sight of us, she jogged over, set the cups down on the nearest gray plastic seat, and enveloped all three of us in a hug that swayed back and forth like a willow in a breeze.

"You two didn't have to come, too, but I'm so glad you did. Did you drive Robbie here? You two are just the best. You really found yourself some good friends this time, Robbie. Guess that new school's not so bad after all, if it has kids like this in it. I'm Allie, by the way. Robbie's aunt. He probably already told you, but I figured I'd introduce myself just in case. You must be Jackson and Leo? It's great to meet you. Do you want some coffee or tea or soda or something? I can go back to the cafeteria and get some—"

"We're fine," I said. "But thanks."

She wrapped her arm around Robbie. "How are you holding up, kid? You see your mom?"

"Yeah." Robbie didn't meet her eyes, his voice forcefully bright. "She went to be with Maya. The doctor said it sounds like she's going to be okay."

Allie's arm tightened around Robbie's shoulders and gave him a firm shake. "Of course she is! It'll take more than a little side-swipe to take out our Maya. That girl's made of steel." She glanced at the TV and looked suddenly crestfallen. "Oh, no, did I miss the wedding?"

"There *was* no wedding," Jackson said in a grim voice. "MaryBeth found out Collin was cheating on her and called it off."

"*What?* No. That jerk!"

"Right?"

Jackson and Allie ended up sitting next to each other facing the TV, talking animatedly about the jerkiness of

Collin. When Allie handed Jackson one of the cups she was holding, he accepted it without hesitation and took a sip of whatever was inside.

I threw Robbie an amused look, but he was staring into the distance with worry and sorrow battling in his eyes. "Hey," I said gently. I ushered him over to two chairs some distance away from the soap opera chatter. "You heard the doctor. Maya's gonna be fine."

"I know."

"That's not what's bothering you."

He shook his head.

I remembered the dream vision of the picnic, Robbie, Maya, and their faceless parents laughing and joking on a picnic sheet. It had probably just been an invention of my mind, but it still had a ring of truth to it. Things had been good between them once, or it wouldn't be so painful for Robbie now.

"Look," I said, "I wish I knew how to make this better for you. I wish there was something I could say, or do, but there just isn't, and that sucks. This whole thing sucks, and it's going to keep sucking until your parents stop acting like idiots and realize how amazing you are. But until that happens, if you ever need a reminder of your general awesomeness, I'm happy to be the one to remind you. Because you are, you know. You're awesome. I've only known you for three days, and I can already see that. And if they can't see it, too, that's their damn loss."

Robbie didn't look at me as I spoke, but something changed in his eyes as my words got more earnest and passionate. When I'd finished, he turned to me with a wondering look and reached up to rest his palm on my cheek, just as he had in the dream. My skin tingled with the touch, and the breath hitched in my chest.

"You're pretty great yourself," he said.

"David!" Allie said loudly, and I thought she was talking about someone on the soap opera until I caught the fear in Robbie's eyes. He pulled away from me and got to his feet, facing a tall, suit-clad man with sandy hair and a brooding face who was currently attempting to shoot lasers from his eyeballs into my skull.

"Dad," Robbie said.

The man's eyes were dark like Robbie's, but there was no warmth in them. He ignored Robbie and turned to Allie. "Where's Charlotte?"

"She's in the room with Maya. They're still running some tests—"

He hurried away to the nurse's station before Allie could say anything more, and after a few sharp words to one of the nurses, he was escorted down the hallway toward whatever room held Maya and Mrs. Welsh in it.

"We should go," Robbie murmured.

Jackson, Allie, and I had all been watching him with equally concerned looks on our faces. We exchanged glances.

"You sure?" Allie asked. "You have just as much right to be here as—"

"I'm sure." Robbie's voice was low. Fractured. "I want to go. Tell Maya we were here?"

"Yeah, of course." Allie didn't sweep us into another hug, but she squeezed Robbie's shoulder and gave Jackson and me entreating looks that clearly said *Please take care of him!* as we headed for the door.

The next thing I knew, we were climbing back into Jackson's car and sitting in the chilly interior listening to an ambulance go screaming off into the distance.

"So, that wasn't great," Jackson said.

Robbie and I didn't answer, but agreement hung heavy in the air.

"You guys want to go back to my place? Mom won't get home until after four."

"School," I said.

"Yeah," Robbie said.

Jackson was silent for a moment, nodding. Then he threw Robbie a quick look over his shoulder. "We have snacks."

There was a soft sigh from the backseat. "Yeah, okay."

Jackson grinned and slid on his shades, and we peeled out of the hospital parking lot in search of a better day.

Chapter Fourteen

Twenty minutes later, we sat together on the worn brown sofa in Jackson's basement, passing bags of chips back and forth and watching some random cartoon all of us were looking at but none of us were paying attention to. Jackson had snagged us root beers from the fridge to wash down the junk food, and it felt good to have carbonated diabetes pouring down my throat while the shoulders of my friends pressed into mine. Robbie still seemed pretty down, but at least he looked a little less devastated than he had at the hospital.

"Should we play a game or something?" I said.

Jackson shot me a dark look. "Dad thinks video games are the devil's playground, remember?"

"No, like, a real game. A board game. Like we used to play when we were kids."

Jackson blinked at me like I'd started speaking another language. "Oh. *Oh!* Yeah, there's a bunch of them up in the attic gathering dust. I'll go get 'em. You guys sit tight, okay? Back in a flash."

Robbie and I were left sitting shoulder to shoulder on

the couch while loud cartoon bangs issued from the TV. I picked up the remote and hit MUTE.

Robbie leaned his head back against the couch cushions and closed his eyes. "Thanks."

There was no sound for a while but a clock ticking somewhere and the distant, rhythmic thud of Jackson's feet climbing the stairs to the second floor of the house.

"I guess I thought something would change," Robbie said into the silence.

I looked at him but didn't speak, letting him find the words. His eyes were open now, fixed on the smooth white ceiling over our heads.

"It's been over a year since they found out, and almost six months since I moved in with Allie. I guess I just thought something would've changed by now, or they would've realized they loved me and nothing else mattered. Stupid, right?"

"Not stupid," I said.

His gaze flickered over to me and then back to the safety of the plaster. "Maya was okay about it when I told her. She was the only one who didn't act like this was some awful thing I'd decided to do, like I was the one tearing our family apart. I don't think she got it, really, but she tried to understand, and she never acted like I was the bad guy. But when Dad told me to move out, she didn't say anything. She just ran upstairs and acted like the whole thing wasn't happening. She didn't stand up for me, she didn't try to talk them out of it, she just let them do it. She never even said goodbye."

I wanted to protest and say that didn't sound like the

Maya I knew, but really, I barely knew Maya, and Robbie had known her for most of his life.

"She texted me a few times after I moved in with Allie, but I blocked her. I was mad, I guess. And then school ended and it was summer, and we didn't see each other at all and that was okay. I tried to pretend I'd always lived with Aunt Allie, and that I didn't even have parents or a sister. It worked, sort of. But every now and then I'd see them when we were out shopping, or Allie would take a shortcut home and we'd pass by my old neighborhood, and I'd just—I'd lose it. I had a lot of panic attacks around then, but Allie helped me through them, got me a good therapist, and things got better.

"And then school started again, and I figured new school, new chance. A fresh start. And there was Maya, right in my first period class. She looked so different I didn't even notice her at first, but when I did, I just wanted to run."

I remembered that class, how Robbie had rushed out without even glancing at me after Mr. Raines dismissed us. I'd thought it had meant he wasn't interested in being my friend, but it hadn't been me he was running from.

"But you know what?" he went on. "It's been good hanging out with you and Jackson and Maya these last few days. I don't know if I've forgiven her, but she's still my sister, and all I've wanted for these last six months has been for things to go back to how they were before. For us to be friends again. It was finally starting to feel like we were getting there when this happened. I just—I wish things hadn't turned out this way. I wish my parents could accept me. I wish Maya had said something when they kicked me out. I wish a lot of things."

I was quiet for a moment, thinking. "How do you know she didn't say anything?"

"What do you mean?"

"I mean, I haven't known Maya for that long, but she stuck up for me in class when Aspen was being awful and transphobic. She wouldn't do that if she had a problem with trans people, right? So what if she did say something to your parents? Before you left, or after? Or what if she wanted to but didn't because she was afraid? She's adopted, after all. Maybe she was afraid that if they could throw out their own flesh and blood, they wouldn't hesitate to do the same to her. I don't know. But if you really want to find out the truth, you should ask her."

He eyed me doubtfully, and I charged on with new certainty.

"Look, I'm sure she had a reason. I don't know if it was a good reason, but whatever it was, you deserve to know it. And maybe she's been wanting to tell it to you but just never had the chance."

Robbie was silent, gazing up at the ceiling. Then he lifted his head and peered at me. "You're pretty smart sometimes, you know."

I gave a twist of a smile. "Just sometimes?"

He sat up and faced me, and my heart gave a little stutter at the realization that we were sitting alone together on the couch, and Jackson was far enough away that I couldn't even hear him moving around anymore. I swallowed and tried to think of something, anything, to say while Robbie's eyes were fixed so intently on mine, but my mind had gone blank, and my heart hammered an unsteady rhythm in my chest.

"Um," I said. "I..."

Robbie scooted forward on the cushions until we sat nose to nose, as near as we'd been in the dream. His face filled my vision, his amber-flecked brown eyes all I could focus on. I had the sudden, mad urge to leap off the couch and run like hell in the other direction.

"You look nervous," he said softly.

"I am."

"Why?"

The truth tumbled past my numb lips. "Because I think you're going to kiss me."

Robbie had been leaning in, but at that he froze. "And you're nervous because you don't want me to?"

My mouth was so dry I could hardly manage to swallow. I shook my head. "Because I'm afraid of how much I want you to."

Robbie's eyes widened, and then his expression settled into a small, determined smile. He lifted his hand to my face for the second time that day. This time, as I had in the dream, I leaned my cheek into his touch and then pressed my hand over his, holding it there and enjoying the warmth of his fingers under mine. He was gazing at me with an intensity I'd never seen in him before, eyes glittering and lips parted. And then he leaned in and pressed his mouth to mine.

It was, for all intents and purposes, my first kiss. It was warm and soft, Robbie's breath whispering against mine as our lips touched. His fingers brushed along my jaw and buried themselves in my hair, and I wasn't sure what to do with my hands, but somehow they figured out what to do and slid over Robbie's shoulders, grazing down his arms and then along his sides. He made a soft sound against my mouth as my palms pressed flat against his back, smoothing over the lump of his binder, and then he was pushing closer, pressing our bodies together as our lips met and parted, met and parted. I leaned back against the armrest of the couch and all but clutched Robbie to me, enjoying the warmth and heaviness of his body on mine, the electric tingles his lips sent thrilling through me.

All too soon, he pulled back, and we stared at each other with our foreheads pressed together, both of us breathless and smiling.

Robbie's gaze ducked shyly away from mine. "Was that…okay?"

I gave a startled choke of a laugh. "Are you kidding? It was amazing."

He grinned, and I took a moment to just look at him, taking in his warm brown eyes, the dusting of freckles over his cheeks, the way one reddish-blond curl hung low over his left eye. Realizing I could, I brushed the curl back from his face, and Robbie caught my hand and brought it lightly to his lips. My skin seemed to catch fire where his lips pressed, and I suddenly wanted very badly to kiss him again. Instead, I pulled him to me and wrapped my arms around him, pulling him close until I felt his heart beating against mine.

We ended up nestled in a warm little ball of arms and

legs on the couch. Robbie's head leaned into mine and mine leaned into his, and I could feel his chest moving as he breathed. All I wanted to do was drift there with him for a few hours, or maybe the rest of my life…

"Hey, how do you guys feel about Battleshi—oh, Jesus Christ."

We untangled ourselves and found Jackson standing on the carpeted basement stairs with an armful of dusty board games and a look of exasperation on his face.

"Seriously? I was gone for, like, five minutes, and this is when you decide to declare your undying love for each other?"

"No undying love has been declared," I said. "We just, uh, got a little bit closer while you were gone."

"Mm-hm." He eyed us doubtfully. "And you, Robert? What do you have to say?"

"I kissed him," Robbie said with a shy but unrepentant glance at me. "But in my defense, I've been wanting to for days and I held back until now, so I think I should at least get some credit for self-control."

Jackson shook his head and dropped the board games onto the coffee table. "Well, at least one of you's willing to be honest." He picked up his abandoned can of root beer and held it aloft. "Mazel tov, you guys. Now, Battleship?"

We spent the day playing board games, drinking soda, eating junk food, and talking. For all that I'd only met Robbie on Monday, it felt like we'd known each other for ages—we laughed and joked with each other like old friends, and as I watched Jackson nearly snort soda out of his nose because he was laughing at something Robbie had said, I knew he felt the same way.

We talked about a lot of things—music, TV, people at school—but Robbie carefully avoided discussing anything connected to his family, artfully sidestepping any topic that could have led the conversation back to them. After meeting his mom and dad at the hospital, I couldn't blame him.

After a while, Jackson even felt comfortable enough to fill Robbie in on his longstanding crush on the goth boy next door, which of course meant we had to run upstairs to Jackson's room and find a picture of said goth boy in the yearbook.

"Not bad," Robbie said as Sebastian Reinhold's black and white face stared out at us from the glossy yearbook page.

I didn't know Seb all that well, as he was a year ahead of us in school, but he was definitely a good looking guy. He had an angular face with high cheekbones and a prominent nose, and the clash of his pale skin with the dark eye makeup and straight black hair was pretty striking. I hadn't been all that impressed with him the few times I'd interacted with him—his entire personality seemed to be summarized by the word "sulky"—but Jackson had been into him for years, so there had to be something more to him than I was seeing.

As Jackson started to close the yearbook, the pages fluttered and he laughed and poked a finger at his own picture. "Oh, man, I forgot how bad I looked in this. God, what was going on with my hair?"

The hair did look a little off, lying ungelled and flat in thick, straight bangs over his forehead, but I barely noticed it. My eyes had gone to another picture on the opposite page.

Jasmine had styled my hair that morning. I remembered sitting in the chair in her room and hearing the sizzle of the curling iron, Jasmine's unconcerned chatter as she pulled long strands of my hair into the iron and released them in graceful ringlets. I'd sat looking at myself in the mirror as she did this, and I remembered a strange, out-of-body sense that I was looking at someone else, that the person I was seeing in the mirror was a stranger instead of my own reflection.

In the picture, though, all I saw was a smiling girl with nicely curled hair and makeup. She looked like any other teenage girl, but she didn't look like me. She wasn't me, and she never had been.

The yearbook closed with a snap. Jackson and Robbie were both watching me, Jackson looking like he wanted to apologize but also didn't want to call any more attention to the whole thing, Robbie with a soft, understanding sympathy in his warm brown eyes.

In the end, I took a breath and said, "So, should we get back to Monopoly?"

The relief from Jackson was palpable, but he covered it by throwing me a sour glance. "Or we could play something else. Something I actually have a shot at winning."

At Robbie's questioning look, I explained, "I have a supernatural ability to win at Monopoly. It's one of my few true gifts."

"It's freaking annoying, is what it is," Jackson grumbled.

"We used to play it all the time when we were kids, and not once—*not once*—did I beat this guy."

"What can I say? I'm the best."

As we followed Jackson down the stairs, Robbie took my hand and gave it a quick, supportive squeeze before releasing it. Some of the tightness in my chest dissipated, and I decided to let the dark memories of my pre-transition life drift back into the past where they belonged.

Robbie ended up winning at Monopoly, and as Jackson whooped and cheered and threw Monopoly money into the air like confetti, I didn't even mind being unseated as champion. Robbie grinned and shook my hand in a show of concession, and as I vowed revenge in a rematch, all I could think was how good it felt to have his hand in mine.

Chapter Fifteen

When Jackson dropped me off at home a few hours later, just after when school would've gotten out, I walked in to find my mother waiting grimly for me at the kitchen table.

"___," she said, "we need to have a talk."

The familiar flutter of terror went through me—Jasmine must have told her after all—but I forced down my fear. Robbie had faced his estranged family today and had even freaking kissed me, and if he could be that brave, then dammit, so could I.

"I know," I said. I walked over to the kitchen table and sat down across from Mom, who had her hands folded on the tabletop and her Serious Face on. "I've been wanting to talk to you about this for a while, but I just could never seem to get it out. But I'm going to do it now."

Mom flinching back from me, disgusted. Mom deadnaming me and misgendering me like Robbie's mom had. Mom saying she could never accept this, would never accept this. Horrified tears shining in Mom's eyes like they had in Jasmine's. The usual dark thoughts swam through my head, but instead of letting them chase me away from this moment, I used them to bring me closer to it. Maybe Mom wouldn't accept me.

Maybe she'd react as badly as Jasmine had, but that didn't change the fact that I had to tell her. The only way past this moment was through it.

I took a deep breath.

"Mom, I'm transgender. I know you think I'm just embarrassed about my 'developing body', but that's not what's been going on with me at all. I don't like showing my body because it's not the body I should have, and that's because I'm a guy, not a girl. It might seem sudden, but it's something I've been thinking about for a really long time, and I know deep down in my heart that it's true. This is who I am. It might be hard for you to accept, but it's the truth, and if you've taught me anything, it's that it's important to be yourself, so that's who I'm going to try to be. I hope you can accept that."

I let out a shaking breath and managed to lift my eyes to look at her face.

Mom gazed back at me with an expression in her dark eyes I couldn't identify.

After what felt like an eternity, she cleared her throat. "Actually, I meant we should have a talk about you skipping school today."

Realization crashed down on me and I sank back into my chair. "Oh," I said in a small voice.

Mom leaned forward and took my hand, and I was relieved to see nothing but love in her eyes. "Sweetie, thank you for telling me. I admit that I wasn't sure what exactly was going on with you, though I knew something was, and this makes a lot of sense. I don't know all that much about transgender people, but if you have any videos I could watch or books you'd recommend, let me know and I'll check them out. You're going to have to be my guide through this, because I want to give you what you need but I won't always know what that is, so you'll have to tell me. Communication, right?"

"Right," I said. To my annoyance, I was crying. Not hard, just a few drips of tears down my cheeks, but crying was definitely happening. "And you don't...you don't hate me? You don't think this is horrible or I'm tearing our family apart or something?"

"Oh, honey, of course not. I know you, and I know you wouldn't say something like this if it wasn't true. You're the only one who can know how you're feeling, and if you say you're a boy, then I can only assume that's what you are. And as for tearing our family apart, if anyone in our family can't handle you being who you are, then that's their problem. If anything, this will be good for us. None of us have ever known a transgender person before, and now here's one living right under our very own roof. Your sisters are going to grow up understanding they should love and support transgender people, and that'll be because of you. And maybe you coming out will finally give Eliza the little push she needs to come out of the closet, though she always has been very private. I just hope she tells us before she and Becky turn eighteen and run off to get married or something."

I couldn't help laughing, and Mom laughed with me. It felt good. It felt amazing.

When the laughter had died down, Mom made a valiant effort at giving me a stern look. "Now, young la—

err, young man. We really do need to have a talk about you skipping school today."

"My friend Maya was in the hospital." Now that I'd finally come out to her, any other words came easily, so easily. "Jackson and I gave her brother Robbie a ride, and some bad stuff happened with his family while he was there, so we spent the rest of the afternoon with him. I know we should've gone back to school, but Robbie needed us, so we just...didn't."

Mom nodded as she absorbed this information. "I see. Well, you should've at least called me and let me know. I could've phoned the school and let them know where you were, and we could've avoided this whole situation. Is your friend Maya all right?"

"Yeah, it looks like. She got hit by a car when she was riding her bike."

"That poor girl! I'm glad she's okay. And your friend Robbie. You said he had some trouble with his family at the hospital?"

I remembered the fear in his eyes when his father walked in, the disappointment when his mother left him behind without a backward glance. "Yeah. Robbie, he's like me. He's trans, and his parents... They don't accept him. They kicked him out, and he's been living with his aunt ever since. They were really awful to him at the hospital."

Mom pressed a hand to her heart and closed her eyes for a moment. "Honey, I'm so sorry to hear that. Well, look, you tell Robbie he's welcome over here any time. In fact, do you want to bring him to your birthday party?"

I blinked at her. "Really?"

Not one trans guy, but *two* at my formal family birthday celebration?

"Of course. And Jackson and Maya are welcome, too, if they want to come, and if Maya's feeling up to it, of course. The more the merrier, right?"

Before I'd considered what I was doing, I was on my feet and circling the table so I could give my mother a tight, squeezing hug.

"Mom, *thank you.*" I felt embarrassingly near tears again and shoved them away as hard as I could. "I was so afraid to talk to you about this, but you're being just ridiculously cool about everything."

When I pulled back, Mom gave me a soft smile and tucked a loose strand of gelled hair behind my ear. "Are you kidding? You're my baby. I'd do anything for you, kid, and accepting you for who you are is just part of being your mom. Your amazing, wonderful mom who is really not feeling like cooking dinner for ten people again tonight."

I laughed. "Fine, fine. I'll do it, but I'm not cooking meat."

"That sounds fair." She headed for the stairs, then paused just short of ascending. "Is there anything else I should know about before I go? Anything else you've been wanting to tell me?"

I paused with the big spaghetti pot halfway out of the cupboard. "Yeah, actually, could you start calling me Leo? That's the name I've been going by with my friends, and at school. I hope you don't think I'm disrespecting you and Dad for not using the name you gave me, but..."

"Leo," Mom said, testing it out. She gave me a soft smile. "It suits you."

She padded up the stairs, and I was left grinning like an idiot in the kitchen, feeling like finally, finally things were going to be okay.

Chapter Sixteen

Maya was back at school the next day, bruised and scraped but waving away our concern. "Guys, I'm fine."

She looked tired, and she told us later that her parents had wanted her to stay home and rest, but she'd insisted on coming to school. They'd driven her as a compromise, as her purple bike had been a bit mangled in the crash and they weren't too keen on her riding it again, anyway.

And now here she was, sitting in first period fending off well-wishers and people who wanted to hear all the gory details.

"They barely touched me, but it was enough to send me up onto the sidewalk and off my bike. I hit my head, I got scraped up, I went to the hospital, but now I'm fine. Really."

"Did you see who did it?" one guy asked. He usually spent class staring out the window and avoiding any kind of social interaction, but now his gaze was locked on Maya's face, a swell of emotion in his eyes.

Maya opened her mouth to answer, then closed it again as her gaze shifted to the classroom doorway. "No, I didn't see who it was. Hey, Aspen."

Aspen Jacobs stood frozen in the doorway, something

oddly like fear in her bright blue eyes. I waited for the insult or the snide comment, but all she said was, "Hey, Maya. Are you, um. Are you feeling okay?"

"Just fine," Maya said. There was a sense of some deeper conversation passing between the two of them, but all Maya said was, "Like I was telling everybody, I'm just a little banged up, but I'm fine."

"Are the police looking for whoever hit you?" Maya's new number one fan persisted. "Because they should be in jail. Like, for a long time."

Aspen paled at this pronouncement, but Maya shook her head.

"No, I'm pretty sure it was just an accident. Whoever did it wasn't trying to knock me off my bike. They might've been trying to scare me, but I don't think they meant to actually hurt me, because like you said, that would be a crime. What do you think, Aspen?"

Aspen gulped something about feeling sick and ran from the room, and Maya sat back in her seat looking pleased. I wasn't entirely sure what was going on, but I had a pretty decent idea, and I also had a feeling that Aspen wouldn't be bothering Maya again anytime soon.

When Mr. Raines came in just before the bell, he smiled warmly at Maya and asked how she was doing, and when he called the roll and Aspen still hadn't returned, Maya kindly said, "She was here, Mr. Raines, but she had to run to the bathroom. I don't think she was feeling very well."

Mr. Raines nodded and made a mark in his gradebook, and by the time Aspen came back, looking a little gray but better, he was in the middle of explaining a particularly difficult proof while the rest of us attended closely and made notes in our notebooks. Aspen sank into her seat and promptly dropped her pencil, which Maya retrieved and held out to her. The look on her face clearly said *Truce?* Aspen stared at the pencil for a long moment, then gave a curt, reluctant nod and accepted it.

Later, when we sat together at the relative privacy of our usual lunch table, I turned to Maya. "So, Aspen was the one who hit you?"

Jackson dropped his fork with a clatter, but Robbie didn't look particularly surprised, having been present for the scene with Aspen in first period.

"Yeah." Maya rolled her eyes like she hadn't nearly been killed the morning before. "She was driving really close to me trying to freak me out, but then it looked like her hand slipped on the wheel and she ended up driving *really* too close."

"And you're sure it was really an accident? I mean, it is Aspen."

Maya gave a little chuckle. "Oh, yeah, I'm sure. You can't fake the kind of terror that was on her face when she hit me. It was definitely an accident, and I'm willing to be forgiving."

"That's important," Robbie said quietly. "Forgiving people."

We all went still. This was the first thing he'd said to Maya since we'd started hanging out together.

Maya looked at him with hope and regret in her eyes. "Yeah. I really think it is."

We finished up lunch and headed to our lockers when the bell rang, and Robbie led Maya over to a quiet corner to talk. I didn't watch or eavesdrop, just grabbed my gym clothes and headed down the hallway with Jackson. I'd managed to get changed in the unisex bathroom and was about to head into the gym when Robbie came sprinting toward me down the hallway. I expected him to stop well before he got to me, but instead he barreled into me in a sort of tackle-hug and spun me around the hallway a few times. By the end of it, we were both laughing.

"Robbie, what—"

"Sorry," he said breathlessly. "I don't know why I did that. I just wanted to."

I laughed again and let myself enjoy the fact that his arm was still around my shoulders, warm and snug. "You talked to Maya?"

"We talked. It turns out she's been trying to get my parents to change their minds this whole time. And back when they kicked me out, she packed up all her stuff and tried to bike to Aunt Allie's—that's why she didn't say goodbye to me, because she was upstairs packing so she could go *with* me. But Mom and Dad caught her before she could go and told her it would be a big imposition on Aunt Allie having two of us staying there, and so she didn't try to go after me again. But she's been sending me texts this whole time. I blocked her number because I was so angry, but she showed them to me on her phone. It's been at least one text every few days since I left. I thought she hated me, but she didn't, not even a little. She's still my sister, and I know that doesn't change how my parents feel, but it's still amazing."

I smiled and, because I could, I hugged him close and tucked my chin over his shoulder. "That's awesome. I'm so glad, man."

"Ahem." We turned guiltily to find Ms. Yamaguchi watching us from down the hall with a volleyball tucked under one arm. "If you gentlemen are finished with your hallway bromance, would you care to join us in the gym?"

"Right," I said. "Sorry, Ms. Yamaguchi!"

"Sorry," Robbie managed.

When she'd gone, Robbie ducked in and kissed me quickly on the lips. I staggered back feeling dazed and knowing I had a ridiculous smile on my face, but he just grinned and disappeared into the bathroom to get changed.

After school, Robbie, Maya, and I piled into Jackson's elderly Toyota, Maya in the front with Jackson and Robbie and me in the back. Jackson hadn't so much asked Maya if she would like a ride home as told her she was getting one, and she'd accepted with a shrug and a grin thrown at Robbie, who grinned right back at her. The conversation as we got underway was light and easy, full of laughter. When I found Robbie's hand and held it in the space between us, he smiled at me and gave my fingers a warm squeeze.

It felt right, the four of us in the car together talking and making jokes, and it wasn't until we were nearly to Maya's place that I realized. We were going to Maya's house. Maya's house, which had once been Robbie's house.

Robbie hadn't said anything in a few minutes, staring out the window with his expression neutral but his jaw muscles taut. My fingers tightened over his reflexively, and he gave a little jolt and turned to look at me as if he'd forgotten where he was. When our gazes locked, I saw it all in his eyes: the fear, the uncertainty, the weary resignation. He knew this was going to hurt him, but he was going to do his best to deal with it anyway, for Maya's sake.

We pulled into a short paved driveway that led to a two-story house with red siding and carefully tended window boxes overflowing with flowers. It was a nice house, well-maintained and one of the best-looking on the block.

As Jackson slid the car into park, there was a silence that should've been occupied with Maya making her goodbyes and hurrying away. Instead, she turned in her seat and looked back at Robbie.

"Okay, hear me out."

Robbie didn't turn away from the window. "I'm not going in there, Maya."

Maya's face was set in determination. "Mom and Dad aren't even home—Dad's at work and Mom has her book club. You never really got to say goodbye to this place, and now might be a good chance to do it. Plus, I have a box of your stuff in my room, and I could really use the extra closet space..." She gave a faint, teasing smile, but Robbie just shook his head.

"Mom and Dad made it pretty clear they don't want me there."

"So? I want you there. It's my home, too, and I'm inviting you and Leo and Jackson to come in and eat some snacks and hang out for a while. Mom's always asking me why I never invite friends over, so really, if you think about it, I'm just doing what she asked."

Robbie looked at Maya properly then, and at the sight of her fierce, determined expression, he sighed and shook his head. "Fine. But don't blame me if this ends in you getting grounded."

"Please." Maya flashed a winning smile and cupped her chin in one hand. "Who could possibly ground this?"

That finally undid Robbie's solemn expression, and he gave a flicker of a smile as he undid his seatbelt with his free hand. "Well, I guess we're doing this." He glanced at me and then Jackson. "You guys okay with this?"

Jackson was already opening his car door. "She had me at 'snacks,' my dude. I'm in."

I smiled and gave Robbie's hand another squeeze. "Me, too."

Robbie squeezed back, gratitude shining in his eyes, and we all got out of the car and headed up the mottled gray stone of the walk. A few steps later, we were on the tidy front porch, facing the door to what had once been Robbie's home.

Maya produced a key and clicked it into the lock, and we stepped inside.

Chapter Seventeen

I stayed at Robbie's side as we entered the house. I could only imagine what he must be feeling, especially since the mere sight of this house had the power to send him into panic attacks in the past. But now that we were inside, he looked oddly calm. The tension had relaxed from his jaw, and he glanced around with detached interest on his face, like this was just another friend's home and didn't hold any special meaning for him.

The interior of the house was dim and smelled like warm cedar. When Maya flicked a light switch, fancy, old-fashioned globe lamps mounted on the walls filled the entryway with a hazy golden glow, and my eyes locked on a framed family portrait hanging on the wall.

Maya and Robbie's parents were dressed formally and conservatively, their mother in a velvety burgundy-colored dress with a high neckline, their father in a gray suit, and Maya and Robbie posed in front of them. The two of them looked to be around eleven or twelve, clad in matching dresses of dark blue velvet with identical silver pendants around their necks.

Maya's dark hair hung in double braids, her hands

clasped in front of her and a bright, glassy smile on her face. Robbie, next to her, was a contrast. His reddish-blond hair tumbled over his shoulders in messy curls, and his body was ramrod straight, his arms held at awkward angles as if he wasn't sure what to do with them. His lips bent in a strained approximation of a smile, but misery pooled in his eyes, a sense of wrongness emanating from every pore of his being. I couldn't bear to look at him for more than a few seconds, and my gaze darted back to the faces of Robbie's mom and dad. They looked so happy and oblivious to Robbie's agony I wanted to slap them both.

I realized we were all standing frozen in the entryway, staring at the picture.

"So," Robbie said, straining to sound casual, "you said something about snacks?"

Maya snapped a smile back onto her face. "Yep! Follow me, gentlemen. The promised snacks await."

She led the way through the hall and into a modern kitchen of stainless steel appliances and marble counters. Maya pulled three different bags of gourmet chips from one of the cupboards, directing Jackson to hunt for sodas in the massive fridge as she did so. Before she could assign me a task, I noticed Robbie wandering through a side doorway into what looked to be the living room.

Plush white couches and armchairs were arranged artfully on a spotless carpet, and I had the same sense of sterility and coldness I'd felt in the hospital. Robbie stood by the red brick of the fireplace, studying a row of small framed pictures on the mantle. He flashed me a small smile over one shoulder.

"Come look at this."

I hesitated, not sure I was even allowed to set foot on the pristine landscape, then went to stand beside him.

He extracted a small, golden-framed photo from where it had been hiding behind the others. When he flashed it at me, I let out a surprised laugh.

It was a school picture of a seven- or eight-year-old Robbie. The background was the standard bluish blur, but Robbie himself was anything but standard. He'd tucked his long curly hair under a baseball cap, giving the illusion of a shorter, more masculine cut, and he wore a black T-shirt with a lightning bolt on it instead of one of the neat blouses featured in the other school pictures lined up on the mantle. The most striking thing about the photo, though, was his face. He was smiling—beaming—looking happier and more himself than in any other photo I'd seen so far.

"I hid the hat and the shirt in my backpack. I didn't put them on until the very last minute, right before I got the picture taken, and the photographer let me do it." His smile softened in memory. "She was really cool. I mean, you can kind of guess someone's going to be cool when they have blue hair and a nose ring, but she really was."

Robbie's smile faded as he tucked the photo back in its place behind the others, and I wondered how his parents had reacted to that picture. Remembering how afraid he had been of his dad at the hospital, I wondered for the first time if his dad had ever hit him, and it made me want to pull Robbie close and never let him go. Instead, I took his hand and squeezed it.

"Snacks?" I asked.

He nodded, and we headed back into the kitchen just in time to hear Jackson say, “No way, you guys have the fancy soda?” He caught sight of me and hefted a can. “Leo, man, check this out. No store brand or anything. This is the real stuff!”

“Only the best in this house,” Maya said in a dry voice.

Robbie and I joined Maya and Jackson at the kitchen table, where I helped myself to a cold can of name brand soda and a handful of gourmet potato chips while Robbie gazed around the room with a thoughtful look on his face.

“There’s something different in here.”

Maya nodded and washed down a mouthful of chips with a swig of cola. “Mom had the walls repainted last month. ‘Extra white’ instead of ‘simply white.’”

Jackson snorted into his soda, and Robbie gave a twist of a smile.

“Dad gave in?”

“Yep.” Maya raised an amused eyebrow at Jackson and me. “Dad wanted ‘super white.’ The argument raged for months before Mom finally won out.”

I glanced uncertainly from Maya to Robbie and back again. “Aren’t those basically the same color?”

Robbie and Maya burst out laughing.

Maya managed to get control of herself first and gasped out, “Months. Literal *months* of them staring at identical paint swatches arguing about which one they should paint this room.”

“It’s not *soothing* enough!” Robbie burst out. “I don’t feel soothed when I look at this color!”

“You don’t need to feel soothed in a kitchen!” Maya

shot back. "You want to feel energized! This white is so much more energizing!"

They both collapsed into laughter again, and for the first time I got a sense of just how close they'd been before their separation. They'd had an entire childhood of shared experiences and shared jokes, and it hit me all over again how unfair it was that their parents' intolerance had driven a wedge between them for so long.

When Robbie and Maya calmed down, Robbie wiping a tear from the corner of his eye, Jackson grinned and got to his feet. "So, are we getting the whole tour of this place, or are we gonna stay here admiring the kitchen walls all day?"

Maya stood and gave a grand gesture with her can of soda. "Oh, absolutely, you will get the full tour! Step right up and follow me, and see what wonders await you."

She led us into a pristine sitting room, a dining room with an elegant wooden table lined with a dark red runner, a study complete with an oak desk, leather armchairs, and a fireplace, and finally to a powder room decorated in pastels and seashell-themed paintings.

"Mom's beachy phase," Maya explained as we ducked our heads in to look. And then we were off again, this time heading up a carpeted staircase to the second floor.

Jackson strode in front next to Maya, playing the prospective home buyer asking questions about load-bearing walls and throwing the term "open concept" into every sentence, while Robbie and I lingered a bit behind. Robbie still looked amused rather than upset, but as we moved down the upstairs hallway, being shown a spacious bathroom, a tidy guest room, and a closet full of towels and linens, his posture grew tense.

"On the left here," Maya said, "is our parents' bedroom, and then here down the hall we have my room and Robbie's room."

A glance into the master bedroom showed a king-sized bed with red satin sheets and a massive dressing table of dark, varnished wood, all sitting on a plush white carpet my family would've stained approximately point-five seconds after its installation. Maya's room was a little way down the hall on the right side, and I couldn't help smiling when she opened the door.

Two of the walls were painted black, and on them were posters of androgynous rockers hanging side by side with framed van Gogh prints. Her bookshelf overflowed with dog-eared novels, most of them science fiction and fantasy, and an actual vintage record player perched atop a cabinet whose glass doors showed an impressive vinyl collection lined up inside.

"Wow," I said, as Maya slid a plug into an outlet and green disco lights started to spin from a little globe on her nightstand. "This is awesome."

Maya grinned as Jackson flopped onto a beanbag chair in the corner of the room and promptly lost the ability to get back up again. "Thanks. It's not bad, is it?"

Robbie still stood near the doorway as if afraid to step too far into the room, or maybe too far into whatever memories it stirred up inside him.

"It's really great," he said. "How'd you get them to let you paint the walls?"

Maya shrugged. "I just painted them. And when Mom painted them back to white, I painted them back to black. Finally Dad got sick of smelling paint fumes all the time and said we had to stop, and so they stayed black after that."

Robbie looked somewhere between wistful and impressed, and I ventured, "They're pretty strict, I guess. Your parents."

Robbie gave a sharp exhale of a laugh. "You could say that."

Maya settled on her bed and wrapped her arms around a stuffed turtle. "They're strict about certain things. Appearance, definitely. Image. They want everything to look 'right.' Dad started out as a janitor and now he's vice president of the company, so it's like he wants to make sure people never look at him or his house or his family and think 'janitor.' He wants them to see this perfect, polished image of him all the time. Especially Mr. Corry."

Robbie turned away, shoulders hunching like he was trying to fold in on himself.

"Who's Mr. Corry?" I asked.

"Dad's boss. President of the company. God, the last time he came over for dinner—" She broke off, her gaze snapping apologetically to Robbie.

Robbie stood at the dresser, fiddling with a small figurine of a bear. He set it down carefully and offered a forced smile over one shoulder. "It's fine. You can tell them."

His voice was strained, and he kept his back to us as Maya, after only a second or two of hesitation, continued her story.

"Um, so, Mr. Corry only comes over for dinner, like,

once a year, but every time he does, Dad gets completely out of control. Everything has to be *perfect*. He hires a maid service to come in and clean the whole house, and caterers to cook these super fancy five-course meals, and he even has people come in and serve us at the table." Her eyes darted to Robbie, then back again. "Anyway, he always likes us to dress up, and this time..."

"I wanted to wear a suit." Robbie turned to face us. Pain welled in his eyes, but he stood straight, a determined lift to his chin. "And he wanted me to wear a dress. And makeup. And 'fix' my hair. We fought about it for days, and finally, at the end of it, when I still wouldn't do it... He told me to get out. 'If you can't do such a simple thing for your family, then you don't deserve to be a part of this family,' I think were his exact words."

I flinched, wondering how often that sentence had echoed in Robbie's head in the months since.

There was a heavy silence.

"You know how worked up he gets about Mr. Corry," Maya said gently. "I bet if he'd had a few days to calm down..."

"He had a few days," Robbie said. "He's had six months."

He opened his mouth like he was going to say more, an angry flush spreading across his face, and then he shook his head and left the room. I exchanged a quick glance with Maya before I followed him. I was sure I'd find him hurrying down the stairs and out to the car, but I was just in time to see him open the door at the end of the hall and slip inside.

I found him sitting on the floor with his knees drawn up to his chest, his head tilted back against the pale blue of the wall. The room itself had clearly once been a bedroom, but now the only signs of it were some faint rectangles on the walls where posters had previously hung.

There was no bed, no dresser, no indication of Robbie having spent years living and sleeping in this room. Instead, there were piles of boxes, shelves stacked with clear plastic storage containers, an exercise bike, a box of holiday decorations. Robbie's bedroom had been converted into a storage room, and if that fact was making my heart twist, I could only imagine how he must be feeling.

Tentatively, I crossed the room and sat down beside him, close enough for our shoulders to touch. It didn't seem right to say anything, so I sat without speaking, a shoulder to lean on if he needed it. A minute ticked by in silence.

Finally, Robbie let out a slow breath. "You know, I think the thing I hate most about all this is that my parents can still hurt me. I don't want them to have that power over me, you know? But they do. Maybe they always will."

I cleared my throat, remembering Robbie consoling me after my talk with my mom. "I guess they can hurt you so much because you love them."

"I don't want to love them. This would all be so much easier if I just didn't care what they thought, but I do. Why do I still care so much?" He waved a hand around the converted store room. "I mean, look at this. They didn't even care enough to keep my room. They clearly didn't expect me to ever come back."

"Do you want to come back?"

"No. But it'd be nice if me completely dropping out of my parents' lives had some effect on them."

"It did." Maya leaned against the doorjamb with her arms folded, her voice soft and her dark eyes locked on Robbie's face. "Mom cried for two weeks. Dad locked himself in his study and we barely saw him except at dinner, and then he just sat there fuming the whole time. They didn't empty out your room because they didn't care—they did it because seeing your stuff in here hurt them too much."

Robbie shook his head. "Then why didn't they ever ask me to come back? Why didn't they apologize, or…"

"Because they still think of this as something you did, not something they did. It would never occur to them that they should apologize to you, because they're waiting for you to come back and say that it was all a mistake and you're really a girl after all, and then everything can go back to 'normal.' In their minds, even though Dad straight-up told you to leave, *you're* the one who left *them*. They see themselves as the victims in all this, the noble, suffering parents who just want what's best for their kid."

Robbie was silent for a beat of five, his eyes blazing. "That is *bullshit*."

"Oh, I know," Maya said. "And I've told them that a thousand times, but they just don't want to hear it. Look, you know they've always loved you more than me, right?"

The anger on Robbie's face was replaced by startled confusion, but Maya continued before he could say anything.

"Which is fine. I know they love me, but it's just

different with you, you know? I mean, they wouldn't have fostered me at all if it weren't for you."

I shot Robbie a puzzled glance, and he gave a weak, bitter smile. "You know how I told you I'm not great with people? It was about a million times worse when I was little. I was scared of pretty much everything, and everyone. I didn't want to go anywhere or talk to anyone. Some psychiatrist my mom talked to said a brother or sister might help pull me out of it, but Mom had already had a hysterectomy after some medical issue when I was born, so..."

"So they decided to foster me." Maya came fully into the room and sat cross-legged on the carpet in front of us. "They loved you so much they brought in a whole other kid just so you wouldn't be alone. I'm not saying they don't love me—I know they do—but you were their first, and there's so much expectation wrapped up in that. If I'd been the one to come out as trans, they wouldn't have liked it, but they would've dealt with it. But you? They had this perfect image in their head of who you were and who you were going to be, and you coming out finally showed them that none of that was real. And instead of getting to know the real you, they're clinging to that image and just hoping you'll 'come to your senses' and go back to being who they thought you were."

"But I'm never going to do that." Robbie's voice was rough with anger and frustration. Loss.

"I know." Maya shook her head sadly. "And I hope someday Mom and Dad will realize that. Otherwise, they're going to get awfully lonely after I graduate, because I'm not coming back here unless you're allowed to come with me. And as yourself. If they won't call you by your real name and use the right pronouns, we're not coming back here, period. I don't care how much Mom lays on her guilt trips, they can have Christmas dinner alone for the rest of their lives for all I care."

There was a pause, and then Robbie launched himself forward and wrapped his arms around Maya, nearly bowling her over with the sudden embrace. They clung to each other for a long time, and when they started murmuring soft words to each other, I got to my feet and slipped out of the room, closing the door behind me. I'd just reached the bottom of the stairs when Jackson strolled in through the kitchen doorway, car keys in hand.

He jerked a thumb in the direction of the front door. "Maya asked me to carry some stuff of Robbie's out to the car. They okay?"

I nodded. "Yeah. Just having a sibling moment."

We settled in at the kitchen table and partook of the chips and fancy soda until footsteps thudded on the stairs. Maya and Robbie appeared in the doorway, arms intertwined and matching looks of warmth on their faces.

"Well," Jackson said, getting to his feet, "I hate to eat all your chips and run, but we probably ought to get going."

"Yeah," Robbie said. "Allie will be wondering where I am. And when I tell her, I'm pretty sure she won't believe it."

Maya walked us to the door, and before we left, she and Robbie shared one more quick, squeezing hug. "Say hi to Aunt Allie for me," Maya said.

"I will. Are you going to tell Mom and Dad I was here?"

"Do you want me to?"

Robbie opened his mouth, then closed it again and gave a soft smile. "No. See you tomorrow."

As we headed for Jackson's car, Robbie stood a little taller, and I wondered if Maya had been right about him needing to say a real, proper goodbye to this house and the life he'd lived in it. The person he'd been when he lived here.

As Jackson revved the engine and got us underway, Robbie leaned back in his seat with a look of contentment on his face, and I knew he was going to be okay.

I didn't find out about Jackson until after we'd dropped Robbie off at his aunt's house. We backed out of the driveway and were turning toward my neighborhood when he let out a long breath.

"So, I got in pretty big trouble with my dad over skipping school yesterday."

I blinked at him, but of course the school had notified his parents, too, and of course they had overreacted. "Did you tell him we were literally taking someone to the hospital?"

He winced and scrubbed a hand over the back of his head. "Yeah, and things got kind of heated and I ended up coming out to him and my mom."

"*WHAT?*"

Jackson jerked the steering wheel and nearly drove us off the road. "Jesus, man, don't yell like that!"

"You *came out* to your parents last night and you're only telling me this now? What happened? Are you okay?"

A little smile played on his lips. "Yeah, so, it turns out my mom had already figured it out, and she told my dad ages ago and they've just been waiting all this time for me to tell them. They're okay with it."

I genuinely could not believe this could be true. "Wait, wait, wait. Your mom—*your mom*—and your dad—*your dad*—are not only okay with you being gay, but they already knew?"

Jackson gave a little shrug and a helpless smile. "Yeah, looks like? I mean, I can tell Dad's not all that comfortable with it, and this does explain why he's been sneaking Bible verses into my comics recently. But Mom's fine with it, and Dad seems to get that it's not something he can change about me, so I guess I'm officially out now? I mean, we'll see what happens the first time I bring a boy home, but we'll cross that awkward queer bridge when we come to it, I guess."

I leaned back in my seat, unable to believe everything that had changed over the course of just the last few days. I'd made new friends, I'd come out to my school, my sister, and my mom, Jackson had come out to his parents and it had somehow, impossibly gone well, I'd had my first kiss… It was ridiculous, all of it, but I couldn't remember the last time I'd felt this good, or more like I was on a road that went somewhere I actually wanted to go.

"So, hey," Jackson said, waggling his eyebrows, "wanna come over and make out with me in front of my parents and see how they handle it?"

"I'd love to, but I've got family dinner, and I think your parents probably still think of me as a girl anyway, so it would probably just confuse them."

Jackson's face fell but quickly brightened. "But, hey, we can always queer it up at your birthday party, right? That should be fun, you and me and Robbie and Maya with your whole family?"

I imagined Aunt Audrey's lip curling in disgust as she stormed out of the party, and I grinned. "I'd like that."

When I got home, Shel was waiting with another list from Mom of things we could fix up around the house, and I settled in to the work with a rare feeling of contentment. There was something really satisfying about leaving things around the house a little better than I'd found them, and Shel was good company. As we fixed wobbly table legs and repaired the lock on a downstairs window, we discovered we were both fans of old school rock and roll, and so Shel ran up to the attic and came back with a dusty old radio, which he promptly tuned to an oldies' station. Steely Dan kept us company while we sanded down the edges of the basement stairs, and we sang loudly along to the chorus of "Sister Christian" until Aunt Audrey poked her head out of the adjoining bedroom and sharply asked us if we could stop.

Shel grinned at me and turned down the radio, and from then on we sang along at a lower volume. As we worked, I wondered again how Shel had ended up with someone like Audrey, but maybe she hadn't always been horrible. Mom had shown me pictures of her and Audrey when they were around my age, and Audrey's smile had been as bright and easy as Mom's back then.

But then, pictures rarely told the whole story, did they? I thought of the photo of Jasmine and me sitting on the porch swing, or the picture of me in the yearbook. No one looking at those photos would see me in them and say, *Yes, this is a person who is wearing these clothes and looking this way because they feel they should, but actually they have secretly felt like something is off about them for years, and very soon they will realize it's because they have been a boy all along.*

When we finished our work on the stairs, Shel straightened and swabbed his forehead with a handkerchief. "That's probably enough for today. Great work today, Leo. You ever want a job in construction in Colorado, you let me know, okay?"

The sound of my name—my true name—echoing in this house from Uncle Shel's lips made me so happy I almost laughed out loud. "I'll keep that in mind."

Chapter Eighteen

The next day, Robbie and I stood in front of room 203 at the start of the lunch break, bagged lunches in our backpacks and voices and laughter echoing to us from beyond the closed door. Jackson and Maya had gone to the cafeteria to collect their own lunches before joining us, and I suddenly wished we'd gone with them instead of venturing ahead alone. I exchanged a glance with Robbie, who was chewing on his lower lip and gripping my hand a little too tightly.

"So I guess we just…go in?" I asked.

"Guess so."

Neither of us moved.

Room 203 doubled as the A/V room, but a little rainbow sign hung on the outside of the door, on which someone had written in colorful bubble letters, "WELCOME TO THE GSA: WE HAVE A GAY OLD TIME." It was all very cheerful and welcoming, but at the same time, I was scared. Why, though? What was there to be afraid of? Most people at school already knew I was trans, and here at least was a room full of people who were likely to be okay with that fact. Plus, even Robbie, who hated interacting with strangers, had had the guts to come here, so if he could do that, surely I could find the willpower to actually open the door and go in.

And yet somehow, I kept not turning the doorknob.

I felt Robbie's gaze on my face. When I turned to look at him, the nervousness in his expression had shifted into a soft, affectionate smile. He brought my hand to his lips, and the usual warm tingle shot through me at the tenderness of the gesture. Affection swelled in my chest, and I had no choice but to use his grip on my hand to pull him close and kiss him. He gave a surprised laugh but leaned in to the kiss, his arms wrapping loosely around my neck. I was just thinking that maybe we could go to the GSA next week instead when someone cleared their throat behind me.

"Well, gentlemen, looks like you're in the right place." Otis gave a burst of his bright, infectious laughter.

I pulled away from Robbie, my cheeks warming. Otis stood in the doorway in an oversized black hoodie that said, *Dinosaurs are cool. Transphobia is not*, and I wondered if he'd worn it today specifically for our benefit. But really, with Otis, who knew? He'd just caught Robbie and me making out in the middle of the hallway, but there was no awkwardness in him at all, just easy laughter as he ushered us into room 203.

The left half of the room was filled with A/V equipment, black, dusty DVD players and sound mixers stacked on carts with wires snaking everywhere, but the right half had been decorated with colorful posters and banners, and a long table sat in the middle of the floor with folding chairs surrounding it. Mr. Brutlag, the other advisor for the GSA aside from Mr. Raines, sat at the teacher's desk at the front of the room, a dog-eared novel in his hands and his feet up on the desk to expose a glorious pair of rainbow socks tucked into his sensible loafers. He grinned and waved at us as we entered, the cover of his novel turning enough to reveal the two men locked in a loving embrace on the front. Another little part of me relaxed.

Almost all the chairs were occupied by talking, laughing students, most of whom I'd seen around school, even if I didn't know their names. At least fifteen sets of eyes fixed on Robbie and me as Otis made his introductions.

"GSA, this is Leo and Robbie. Leo and Robbie, this is the GSA."

Robbie and I raised our hands in weak waves of greeting, and a cacophony of voices raised to say things like "Hey!", "Welcome!", or "Nice to meet you!"

Otis grinned like this was all going according to plan and led us to two free spots at the table, next to a girl with straight, bubblegum-pink hair and a heart-shaped face. She smiled and accepted a kiss on the cheek from Otis as he passed, and a boy sitting across the table made a face.

"Ew, gross, straight people." He put his hands to his cheeks in mock-horror, and Otis and his girlfriend both laughed.

Otis turned back to Robbie and me and waved a hand at the pink-haired girl. "Boys, this is my favorite human. Favorite human, these are boys."

The girl rolled her eyes. "You're such a weirdo, Otis."

He grinned. "You love it."

And it was clear she did, although she gave him another

impressive eye roll as he wandered away to talk to some people at the other end of the table. Robbie and I sat motionless in our chairs, not sure what we were supposed to be doing, until Otis's girlfriend gave us a warm smile.

"You guys nervous?"

I gave an awkward laugh. "Is it obvious?"

She took a sip from a bottle of water sitting on her lunch tray. "Not really, but most people are when they first come here. Especially if they're not really out yet."

I glanced at Robbie. Were we out?

"I'm Kenzie, by the way. Otis can be kind of a lot sometimes, so if you have any questions, you can always ask me. Or anyone, really. Everyone here's pretty nice."

Robbie was cautiously extracting his bagged lunch from his backpack, not looking quite so much like he wanted to bolt, so I took a breath and unzipped my own bookbag.

"So, what do you guys usually do here?" Robbie asked.

Kenzie shrugged. "Usually we just hang out, eat lunch, and have a good time. We're planning some events for Coming Out Week in October, and we've been trying to get the principal to let us do the Day of Silence this year, but mostly it's just this." She waved a hand at the lunch table and its inhabitants.

I opened my mouth to ask why they even bothered having a club if they didn't do much of anything, but the words died in my throat as I glanced around the table. Two boys gazed adoringly into each other's eyes, two girls held hands on the tabletop, a boy slid mascara onto his lashes while holding a conversation with a tall, glamorous girl with aquamarine hair, and there were several people with hair and clothes that didn't fall neatly into "male" or "female" categories. They all looked happy here, and completely comfortable. The rest of the world might be a scary place for people like us, but here, we could be ourselves without fear. It was such a small thing but also a huge, huge thing at the same time.

I smiled and exchanged glances with Robbie, and he took my hand on the tabletop and squeezed it. This time, I was the one who brought his hand to my lips and kissed it.

Kenzie hid a smile behind her water bottle. "You guys are adorable."

I had to concede that maybe we were.

Jackson and Maya joined us a little while later, and predictably, they fit right in with the GSA and were soon laughing and joking with the other members as easily as they laughed and joked with us. Jackson and Otis somehow got into a pun-off that involved telling their worst dad jokes and seeing who could get the loudest groan from the onlookers, and Maya ended up debating video games with a girl named Rey who had short, spiky dark hair and impressive biceps.

Robbie and I chatted a little with Kenzie, and after a while, Otis brought another girl over and settled her in the seat between Kenzie and me, saying he thought we would "get along." Nami's hair hung down to her chin in shiny chestnut waves, and her voice was low and warm, her smile easy. We talked about unimportant things for a little while—what classes we were in, what we liked to do one the weekends—and then Nami gave a small, secret smile.

"So, I'm guessing you guys are trans, based on the fact that Otis brought me over here?"

I choked on my water, and Robbie blinked at her in surprise.

"Uh." I coughed the last of the liquid from my lungs. "Yeah, actually."

Nami gave a melodic laugh. "I thought so. Get the trans kids together so they can bond about being trans, classic Otis. He really does mean well, though. He wants everybody here to feel comfortable, and I guess he thought having me talk to you would make you guys feel more welcome."

"We do," Robbie said, then flushed and stared down at his lunch like he'd said too much. "Feel welcome, I mean."

"Yeah," I agreed. We'd only been here for twenty minutes, but I already felt safer than I did in any other place in the school, plus free to stare at Robbie and hold his hand as much as I wanted, which was a definite plus.

Nami's smile softened. "I'm glad. So, do you think you guys'll be back next week?"

I glanced at Robbie, and he gave a warm smile.

"Definitely," I said.

I left the GSA meeting feeling energized and supported, and somehow facing down the stares, whispers, and nastier comments in the halls was easier knowing there was a whole group of people who accepted me without question. Yeah, some random guy in the hallway might be calling me a "fag" (I felt like he was a little confused about what a trans guy even was, but whatever), but there was Otis waving me over to his locker to tell me about some cool new game he'd started playing, or there was Nami joining her arm in mine and drowning out the antagonistic voices with her warm chatter and laughter.

In English class, Mr. Brutlag kept a careful eye on Robbie and me, alert for any potential threats. When one of the basketball guys scoffed at me being chosen to read as Romeo for our class reading of Romeo and Juliet, Mr. Brutlag immediately assigned him the role of Juliet's nurse and sat smiling sweetly at the guy's discomfort at being assigned a "woman's part." It didn't stop the nasty looks being thrown my way, but it did send a definite message that this was a safe space for me and people like me, which I deeply appreciated.

All things considered, I was feeling pretty good by the time we walked into Choir at the end of the day. I'd only taken a few steps into the room, however, when Mr. Tyler called me into his office with an odd look on his face. His little office adjoined the choir room, but it was soundproofed just like the rest of the music wing, giving it the feeling of a bubble about to pop when he closed the door.

He didn't quite look me in the eye as he sat down at his desk. It was crowded with knick-knacks and stacks of sheet music. "Er, so I've been doing some thinking, and I'm wondering if maybe I made a mistake placing you in the baritone section. I was wondering if you might not be more comfortable somewhere else."

Realization dropped like lead into my stomach. "I'm pretty comfortable being a baritone, Mr. Tyler."

A pained look crossed his face as he shuffled the papers on his desk. "It's just that I'm not sure you'll be able to reach some of the lower ranges we expect baritones to reach, and so maybe you'd be better off in tenor, or…"

"Or alto?"

He stared down at his desk and nodded.

In the past, I might have shrunk away, quietly acquiesced, or just quit choir altogether. But things had changed. I had changed.

"Mr. Tyler, you listened to me sing on Tuesday, and you decided then that based on my voice and my range, I belonged in the baritones. Has my voice changed since Tuesday?" I took a step closer, my jaw tightening. "Or did you maybe find out something that made you think of me differently? Because I'm still the same person. I'm the same guy, with the same voice, and I'm not leaving the baritones."

Mr. Tyler still didn't meet my eyes. "I understand how you feel, but I have to do what's best for this choir."

"What's best for the choir," I echoed.

My fingers shook, but I still tugged open the office door and called for my fellow baritones to join us. He wanted to do what was best for the choir? Fine. Let him ask the choir, then. The baritones had been chatting and laughing in our usual spot, but they filed into the room and frowned at a gaping Mr. Tyler as I closed the door behind them.

"So, guys." I took a deep breath and forced myself to meet their eyes as I spoke. "Mr. Tyler thinks I should leave the baritone section and go into tenor or alto instead, and I wanted to know what you thought about that."

I hoped at least one of them would speak up in my

defense. What I didn't expect was the immediate outcry from every single one of them.

"What? Lose Leo the Lion?"

"We finally get another baritone, and you're taking him away after *one day*?"

"You can't do this to us, Mr. T. The tenors get all the good singers, and don't even get me started on those damn altos..."

"Baritones forever!"

It went on for a while, during which time one of the guys, a cool, punk rock-ish blond guy named Noah, wrapped his arm protectively around my neck in a half-headlock, half-hug that might've been uncomfortable if it hadn't meant so much to me.

Finally, Mr. Tyler got to his feet and waved his hands at them. "All right, all right, fine. You've made your point." He looked at me properly, at last, and gave a grudging nod. "You've made your point. Leo can stay in the baritones."

The baritones roared their approval, Noah giving my hair a cheerful ruffle as he released me from the headlock. I left Mr. Tyler's office surrounded by happy, laughing baritones, feeling light on my feet and even lighter in my heart.

The light feeling was still with me when I got home that afternoon and Mom and I sat down in Maribel and Eleanor's bedroom facing my three youngest sisters. With my permission, Mom introduced the concept of trans people to them, then turned to me and let me tell them that

I was trans and what that meant for how they should address me.

Eliza took it all in with her intelligent dark eyes, nodding and making notes in the little notepad she always seemed to have with her. Maribel and Eleanor didn't look as interested, but when I'd finished speaking, Eleanor raised her hand like we were in school.

"So, instead of being our sister, you're our brother?"

"Right," I said.

Eleanor looked at Maribel. Maribel looked at Eleanor.

"Okay," they said, and that was that.

The adults, I knew, would be a harder sell, but Shel was still calling me by the right name as we continued our handyman tour through the house, and Grandpa had somehow picked up on it and was now calling me "Leo" no matter how many times Grandma or Aunt Audrey tried to correct him. It finally seemed like enough of my family knew or almost knew that it was probably time to just come out to all of them and deal with the consequences.

We did it after dinner that night, when everyone was gathered in the living room listening to Maribel and Eleanor chattering about what they'd done at school that day. Mom and I waited until they'd concluded with, "And it was the funnest day ever," and then Mom got to her feet to make a formal address.

"So, there's something we'd like to talk to you all about." She used her best strong, clear, and confident Business Voice, and everyone quieted immediately. "But it's not my news to tell, so I'll let our Birthday…Individual give you the details."

She shot me an apologetic smile, I assumed because of "Birthday Individual," but I was mainly just touched she was trying so hard not to either misgender me or out me before I'd had the chance to tell the family myself.

The full weight of everyone's attention fell on me, and I fought back a burst of stage fright. The only person not looking at me was Jasmine, who was staring angrily down at her feet.

"So, you've probably noticed I've changed some things about how I look lately," I said. "I cut my hair at the beginning of the summer, and I've been wearing different clothes and acting more like…well, like myself. Yes, Maribel?"

Maribel dropped her raised hand back into her lap. "Is this about you being transmember again?"

I laughed, and Mom did, too. "Yes." I looked at Grandma Pearl, Uncle Shel, Aunt Audrey, and then at Grandpa Earl's vague but contented smile. "So, I don't know how much you guys know about transgender people, but that's what I am. It basically means that while I might look like what we usually call a 'girl,' I'm actually a boy. My body says 'girl' but my heart and my soul say 'guy', basically."

"And what this means," Mom slid in smoothly, wrapping her arm around my shoulders, "is that we've been using the wrong name and pronouns for a very long time, and it's well past time we stopped." A sheen of tears glistened in her eyes as she smiled at me. "This is my son, Leo. I'm proud of him, and I'm so happy he finally feels comfortable enough to be himself with us."

A brief silence fell, and then Uncle Shel got to his feet

and held out his hand for me to shake. Grandma Pearl came over looking confused but nevertheless gave me a hug and said, "I'll try to get used to it, but my memory isn't so good these days, you know," and Grandpa Earl just sat humming to himself but winked at me when he caught me looking. And then Maribel and Eleanor were dancing around my legs with their arms linked singing, "We have a bro-ther, we have a bro-ther," and Eliza jumped to her feet and said, "Mom, I think I'm gay!" and it was beautiful pandemonium until Jasmine slammed the lid of the piano down with a crash.

We all froze. Jasmine stared at us with tears in her eyes, her hands clenched into fists at her sides. "How can you all be okay with this? How can you think this is okay? This is *not okay!*"

She ran from the room, and her feet pounded up the stairs. Mom started to go after her, but it was Aunt Audrey—who hadn't said anything after my announcement and had instead been hanging back with her lips pressed into a thin line—who got to her feet and said, "I'll go talk to her."

Audrey left without waiting for Mom's answer, and gradually noise and life returned to the living room. The twins turned their mirth to Uncle Shel and started dancing around his legs instead, Eliza approached Mom to talk about her upcoming nuptials to Becky, I assumed, and Grandma Pearl sat by Grandpa Earl patting his knee and assuring him it wasn't quite time for the news yet but we would definitely watch it when it came on. Since all I could think about was the hurt and betrayal on Jasmine's face as she ran past me, I slipped out of the room and up the stairs.

I hadn't intended to eavesdrop, but Jasmine's door was open a crack. As I paused outside to consider whether or not I should knock, a voice I didn't recognize floated out to me.

"—and I used to dream about what I would name them."

It was Audrey, but her voice was soft and sad and full of real feeling, so unlike the cold tones she usually used.

"I was going to have a daughter named Violet, and then a son named Oliver, and if another one came along after that, they were going to be Alexander or Alexandra, depending. But one day I went to the doctor, and she told me I wasn't going to be able to have any children. Not ever."

She let out a soft breath that trembled with emotion. "I was devastated. Shel was wonderful and supportive—he always is—and said we could adopt, we could foster, we could use a surrogate, but I didn't want to hear any of it. I had a dream of what I wanted to happen, and when it didn't work out the way I wanted, I just shut down. I ignored all the ways I could've been a mother because they didn't line up with what I'd always dreamed would happen."

I couldn't see Jasmine, but I heard a rustle like she was shaking her head. "Aunt Audrey, why are you telling me this?"

"Because I know what it's like to think you have everything figured out and then have it all come crashing down on you. Your mom's been telling me for years how close you and your sister are. Like best friends, she said."

"We used to be." Jasmine's voice was low and bitter.

"But now, I don't know what we are. I feel more like we're strangers."

A hint of the old hardness came back to Audrey's voice. "Sometimes things don't work out the way you think they're going to. But if you hold on to the dreams that can never come true, you miss the happiness that's right in front of you. Shel and I could've been parents. We could've been happy with our kids this very minute, but I wouldn't let us. And you. You still have your sister. She's still there, no matter what she's wearing or what name she's using. You don't have to lose what you have with her, you just have to…adjust your expectations."

There was a long silence, and then Jasmine sniffled. "You know, you could still have kids, Aunt Audrey. You could still adopt, or do one of those other things."

Audrey laughed a little, not the merry, fake laugh but a low, self-deprecating chuckle. "I don't know, I feel like that would be a cruel fate to put on anyone, having me for a mother. But it's something to think about, isn't it? And I have to admit, being here with all of you makes a good case for it. It's something special, isn't it, having a big, happy family?"

"Even when we're not so happy?" Jasmine asked.

"Especially then," Audrey said.

I slipped away from the door and went back downstairs.

Mom met me in the kitchen, her eyebrows lifting in concern. "Is everything…?"

"Not yet," I said. "But I think it will be."

She wrapped her arm around me and gave me a quick, squeezing side-hug. "Come on, let's head back in there.

Maribel and Eleanor managed to talk Shel into playing Clue with them, and I think he could use some moral support."

I grinned, and we walked together into a room full of voices, laughter, and warmth.

Chapter Nineteen

That night, I stood in front of the endless row of dream doors and waited for Dad to show up. It had been surprisingly easy to make the doors appear—I'd visualized them, believed they would be there, and they had been—but the act of summoning them hadn't likewise summoned Dad, and now I wasn't sure what to do. I'd been hoping for another lesson in dream-walking—or, to be honest, just another opportunity to spend time with my dad, even if he was probably a figment of my imagination—but time slipped by and there was no sign of him.

After a while, my thoughts drifted to the non-dream-ghost members of my family, and the infinite line of doors shivered, blinked, and reformed into a set of nine doors. I got to my feet and studied them with interest. One was a sturdy door made of golden-brown wood, with a worn toolbelt hanging from a nail on its back, while next to it was a delicate pair of French doors with frosted windows, elegant but not letting any prying eyes look inside. Shel and Audrey.

I scanned the line of doors, curiosity drawing me forward to examine each one. Eliza's door was covered in

"KEEP OUT" notices, so much so that I wondered if she'd even be willing to let me in, and while Eleanor's and Maribel's doors were both plastered with brightly colored stickers and animal-shaped decorations, Eleanor's were more chaotically arranged while Maribel's were in neat, straight rows.

Mom's door was made of smooth, dark brown wood, complete with a WELCOME mat at its base, while Grandma Pearl's was an old-style door with a big brass knob and matching knocker, intimidating and old-fashioned but basically welcoming. Grandpa Earl's was similar, wooden and with a brass door knocker, but I realized after frowning at it for a few seconds that it was missing a door knob. I drew my fingers along the slight rise in the wood where the knob had once been before I stepped away.

Since Dad was still MIA, I figured I might as well knock on some doors. I started with Maribel and was let in almost immediately. She was laughing on the back of a pony with Eleanor, the two of them flying through a brilliant blue sky as the pony flapped its wings and occasionally burst into song. I expected something similar when I slipped through Eleanor's door, but she was in cartoon safari gear at some kind of archaeological dig site, plucking fossils from the ground and showing them to a smiling boy around her age. Maribel was nowhere in sight. Interesting.

Shel's door was as welcoming as I'd thought it would be—my knuckles had barely hit the wood before the door swung wide open. Inside, Shel was building a house in the sunshine with three kids ranging in age from eleven to sixteen or seventeen. Their faces were blurred like Robbie's parents' faces had been, but I could sense their smiles and how much they were enjoying working with Shel. They called him "Dad" and laughed and joked with him as they hammered nails and worked together carrying long planks of wood, and I closed the door quietly so as not to intrude on the moment.

I knocked on Audrey's door more than once, but it stayed firmly closed and locked. And hey, if my dream version of Audrey wanted to keep me out, that was fair enough. I didn't even try knocking on Eliza's door, and I'd been purposely ignoring Jasmine's door at the far end, so that left me with Grandma and Grandpa or Mom.

Curiosity made me knock on Grandpa Earl's door. I figured nothing would happen, but the door gave a little groan and opened a few centimeters. I tried to push it inward, but the base of the door kept getting stuck as I pushed it. In the end, I was able to shove it open just far enough so I could squeeze inside, and then all I could do was stare.

It was both dark and light, day and night. Lighting flashed somewhere above, and voices echoed all around me, a jumble of words and ideas and emotions. I caught glimpses of faces, snatches of conversations, but they faded as soon as I tried to focus on them. And in the center of all this was Grandpa, seated at his woodworking desk in a circle of lamplight, whittling and looking content as chaos reigned around him. I approached his desk cautiously, not sure if he would notice me or how he would respond if he did.

He didn't look up as I stopped in front of him, but I

was close enough now to see he was whittling a little wooden figure of a man. He held it up to the light and squinted at it, then gave a small smile.

"Looks pretty good, doesn't it?" His watery blue eyes met mine with more lucidity than I was used to seeing in them. "Didn't look like this when I started, but now it's looking like a perfect little figure of a man." To my surprise, he held the figure out to me. "Thought you might like it."

The figure fit perfectly in my palm, the wood warm under my fingers. "You made it for me?"

"I made it and you're here, so it's for you." He sat down and picked up another small block of wood. "I wonder who this one'll be for?"

Grandpa set to work as if I was no longer in the room. All around us, lightning flashed and voices whispered and shouted and laughed, but Grandpa was safe from it all, quietly whittling at his desk.

I backed away and slipped out of the dream, and the door clicked shut behind me.

I peeked into Grandma's door after that and found a much younger version of her in a little house with shag carpeting and wood paneling on the walls. She was chasing two little girls who ran shirtless while shrieking with laughter, but no matter how fast she ran or how she dodged, she couldn't seem to catch them. She was laughing, too, but tired lines creased her mouth and her eyes were sad, as if she wished the two would slow down for just a second so her reaching hands could connect. The girls were always too fast for her, though, and the chase continued.

Finally, there was only Mom's door left. I knocked and

waited, expecting it to swing open as widely and welcomingly as Shel's had, but there was a feeling of hesitation before the lock clicked and it crept open an inch or two.

I slipped inside—and froze.

It was a moonlit night. Insects buzzed, and a warm heaviness hung in the air. Mom stood in the distance in a flowing white sundress I'd seen her wearing in old pictures, and standing in front of her was my dad.

"—so hard sometimes," Mom was saying. Tears were thick in her voice, and Dad's expression was tender as he stroked her cheek. "I'm trying so hard to be strong for them, but sometimes I have to just lock myself in my room and cry. I miss you so much…"

Although the door had opened for me, I felt like an intruder and immediately slipped back out and into my dreamscape.

After that, I let the doors vanish back into the blueness and thought about how maybe Dad wasn't here with me now because I wasn't the only one he was visiting. In the end, I slipped into a deeper sleep and the dreamscape faded, but what I had seen stayed with me, and it was still with me when I woke up.

Mom drove us to the mall early the next morning. While I always enjoyed my drives with Jackson, it was kind of nice to be sitting on the clean, comfortable seat of Mom's Taurus listening to cheerful pop songs at a non-ear-splitting volume. The car smelled fresh and lemony and just faintly of vanilla, and with the Saturday morning sunlight warming me through the windshield, I felt comfortable and content.

I stole glances at Mom as we drove, caught on the memory of her tearful voice in the dreamscape as she gazed at the ghostly figure of my dad. I debated with myself for a while and then cleared my throat. "Um, so, you know you can talk to me if things are ever bothering you, right?"

She cast me a surprised glance that settled into a quizzical frown. "Do you think I'm bothered about you being transgender? Because I promise you, I'm not. It was a surprise, and it might take some time before I'm using the right name and pronouns all the time, but—"

I shook my head hurriedly. "No, that's not what I meant. I just mean… It's got to be hard for you, raising all five of us and working and doing all of it by yourself. So if you ever need, like, to talk, or if you need me to help with something… Well, I'm here."

Mom's expression softened, tears glimmering in her eyes before she blinked them away. Her hand found mine beyond the gearshift and squeezed. "I appreciate that, I really do. And you already do help me, you know. Not just with chores and cooking and things, but with your sisters. I don't know how we would've gotten through the last few years without you. So don't sell yourself short, okay?"

I squeezed her hand back. "You either."

As we continued the drive, the glow of the sun and the comfort of my mom's presence left me warm and drowsy.

"Don't fall asleep," Mom warned as we started up the hill to the mall parking lot. "I don't know anything about shopping for suits, so you'll need to be conscious if you want to find the right one."

I took a sip from my travel mug. Earl Grey coursed through my veins and made everything seem a little brighter. "I won't fall asleep. And this is my first time shopping for a suit, too, you know. What makes you think I know what I'm doing?"

Mom pulled us into a parking spot and gave a secretive smile as she turned off the engine. "Well, lucky for you, I happen to know a few experts who might be able to help us."

We got out of the car, and my eyes widened at the sight of Mr. Raines and a tall, smiling man waiting by the entrance to the mall. Mr. Raines was wearing a yellow sweater and bell-bottomed khakis instead of his usual teacherly ensemble, and the man next to him—dark hair, beard, and a friendly assemblage of laugh lines—wore a light jacket, a black T-shirt with a band logo on it, and jeans.

As we got closer to them, Mr. Raines leaned in to say something to the man, and they both approached us with smiles and waves that made their matching wedding bands glint in the sun.

"Thank you so much for meeting us up here!" Mom shouted over the wind. "We really appreciate it."

"Anything to help a fellow Leo." The man by Mr. Raines held his hand out to me, and my fingers were enveloped in a warm, friendly grip. "I hope you don't mind me coming along, but I thought it might be helpful to have someone here who likes clothing from this century."

"Leo," Mr. Raines said to me, his lips twitching into a

smile, "meet Leo. And just because something is modern does not mean it's better."

Leo tucked his hands into his jacket pockets and grinned. "I'm just saying, no need for this poor guy to get trapped in the seventies just because you are."

"Well," Mr. Raines said smoothly, "should we go inside?"

We left the wind whipping behind us and slipped into the warm, bright interior of the mall. I was a little afraid it might be awkward shopping with my mom, my teacher, and his husband, but Leo and Mr. Raines were completely at ease, laughing and joking and even getting my mom to do her snort-laugh at one point. Before even ten minutes had gone by, it felt like the four of us had been going on shopping trips together for years instead of just minutes.

We visited a few different menswear stores and browsed the merchandise, but in the end, it was Mr. Raines who spotted the suit I would wear for my birthday.

"What do you think of this one?" he asked, and I made way through the racks of dark fabric to examine his find.

It was a gorgeous suit. I would've been happy in just about anything that made me look like the guy I was, but this was the first suit I'd seen that made me immediately think, *Yes, I want to wear that.* It was blue, for one thing, rather than black or dark gray, and I loved the cut of it, the soft but sturdy feel of the fabric, the intricate silver buttons and the slim cut of the pants.

"I love it," I said.

By that point, Leo and my mom had come over to join us, and Mr. Raines cast a subtly triumphant glance in Leo's direction. Leo smiled and shook his head, and I was ushered into the changing rooms by a helpful shop lady with a strip of measuring tape hanging around her neck.

I'd been worried about the fit of the suit, but when I turned to face myself in the mirror, all I could do was stare.

Looking back at me through my reflection was a good-looking dude in a suit. His brown eyes were a little wide with surprise, but he had a nice, square-jawed face with a hint of facial hair over his lip, and his dark hair was styled and gelled so it swooped back from his forehead and then down to tuck behind his ears. He was wearing a suit, and he looked good in it. The blue fabric sat beautifully flat over his chest, and while the cuffs were a little long, stopping at the crook of his thumbs instead of at his wrists, he wore the suit like he belonged in it, like this was what he'd been meant to be wearing all along.

"Leo, you okay in there?" It was my mom, and this was so close to what Jackson had said when I was trying on my binder in the school bathroom that I couldn't help laughing.

"Yeah, I'm fine," I called back. "Just getting the tie on."

"Do you know how to tie a tie?"

I'd watched a bunch of YouTube tutorials and had tried practicing with a scarf, but the actual object was somewhat more difficult to maneuver, particularly when I was in a small dressing room with my mom, Mr. Raines, and his husband waiting for me outside.

I didn't do a fantastic job of it, but I managed to make the tie at least look presentable, and then I took another deep breath and opened the changing room door.

Mom's hand went to her mouth when she saw me.

"Oh. Oh, honey. You look so handsome." She gave a teary smile. "So much like your dad."

Mr. Raines and Leo beamed at me like proud uncles.

"It really does suit you," Mr. Raines said.

"Was that a pun?" Leo asked with a sideways glance. "Seriously, though, Leo, it looks great."

"Honey, how do you feel?" Mom asked.

The shop lady was eyeing me approvingly and tugging on the sleeves, saying something about getting them shortened, but all I could think about was the confident, good-looking guy I'd seen in the mirror.

"I feel amazing," I said.

Chapter Twenty

I spent that afternoon with Robbie. I considered biking to his house but ended up taking the bus instead, as Maya's accident was still a little too fresh in everyone's minds. Mom insisted on kissing me before I went and saying, "Have a nice time, my sweet boy," which was a very nice gesture but also kind of embarrassing since she did it outside on the front porch. I just laughed and wiped the lipstick off my cheek, and soon I was stepping off the city bus and heading up the walk to the little white house where Robbie and his aunt lived.

Knocking on the door made me think of the dream—a picnic, a quiet classroom, Robbie's hand on my cheek—but I pushed the thoughts away and tried to school my face in case Allie answered the door.

It was Robbie who smiled out at me when the door swung inward.

"Hey," he said.

"Hey," I said.

We both laughed a little awkwardly, and Robbie stepped back to let me in.

The interior of the house was warm and cozy, a small

living room on the left with a flowered sofa, coffee table, and TV, a dining room on the right with a round wooden table littered with papers and books. The house's wallpaper was a cheerful combination of white and yellow, and there were little wooden knick-knacks everywhere, plus a friendly orange housecat who rubbed against my legs before taking off for parts unknown.

"So, uh, this is the house." Robbie ducked his head, looking self-conscious, so I made sure he could see my smile as I looked around.

"It's great," I said.

He smiled and led me down a short hallway, past a partly closed bathroom door, and into a small but functional kitchen. "Do you want something to drink, or…?"

"Nah, I'm good. I brought some water."

We stood in silence for a few seconds, then both laughed again.

"So, is your aunt home?"

"No, she had to go out for a little while, but she'll be back in an hour or two."

I glanced around uncertainly. "Is it okay that I'm here, you know, while she's not?"

"Yeah, it's fine," he said, in a way that asked, *Why wouldn't it be?*

And it probably was fine. It wasn't like we were going to somehow get each other pregnant or something, but I couldn't help feeling like I was doing something wrong, being all alone with the boy I was dating while no adults were on the premises. And while Robbie and I had been alone together before, we'd never been quite *this* alone, and

I had no idea if I'd be able to come up with enough non-idiotic things to say to fill an entire afternoon.

Robbie was studying my face, his hands tapping together nervously like they had at the hospital. "Look, if you feel weird about this, or if you'd rather come back later when Allie's home…"

I pushed away my weirdness and went to stand next to him. "No. Really, this is great. Sorry, I just don't know how to be a functioning human sometimes, but I do want to be here. With you."

A shy smile touched his face, and he took my hand. His grip was warm and comfortingly solid as he pulled me toward the door at the far end of the kitchen. It wasn't until we were inside that I realized it was his room, and I looked around with undisguised interest.

It was both what I'd been expecting and not at all what I'd thought it would be. It was small, of course, probably a room meant to be an office rather than a bedroom, but it was cozy rather than cramped. There was a bed against the wall—unmade, a tangle of sheets topped by a blue comforter—and under the window was a small wooden desk with a wobbly looking chair. A few sketchbooks lay on the desktop, and a white CHICAGO mug overflowed with colored pencils and pens.

The walls were your standard off-white, but sketches had been pinned up all over them, some in color and some in black and white. There were trees, people, fruit, the night sky, and a beautifully shadowed drawing of a guitar, the real life version of which was leaning in the far corner of the room. I didn't know anything about guitars, but I got the impression this one had seen a lot of use. Light scratches decorated the glossy golden-brown surface, and the shoulder strap was worn and starting to fray. A little plastic cup sat nearby with a rainbow assortment of guitar picks.

This was Robbie's room, and it was such a *Robbie* space I couldn't help smiling.

"Did you draw all these?" I asked.

He nodded, his cheeks flushed.

"They're amazing," I said fervently. I was about to say more when my gaze caught on a square piece of paper stuck to the closet door like an afterthought. It was another sketch: A grassy meadow, a red picnic sheet, and a mother, father, and two kids laughing and eating together in the sunshine. Just like in my dream, the features of the parents were blurred while the kids were in sharp focus. I glanced back at Robbie, my mouth dry and the back of my neck tingling. It was probably just a coincidence, but what a freaking coincidence.

"It's my family," Robbie said with an embarrassed duck of his head. "We used to go have picnics in the park when Maya and I were little."

I trailed my fingers gently over the paper. "Why are your parents' faces so blurry?"

Robbie slid his hands awkwardly into his pants pockets and shrugged. "I guess because I don't really remember what they looked like back then. They were younger, and happier, but any time I try to draw them, all I can think of is who they are now. All I can see is…not that. Not happiness. So I don't draw their faces. It's easier, too, not to have that reminder of who they used to be."

He sat on the edge of his bed, and I joined him. I wanted to ask him when his parents had changed, when this happy family had self-destructed, but I didn't know how to do it without hurting him more. So I stayed quiet, and after a moment, he tossed me a crooked smile.

"Sorry. I know you must be getting tired of me being all angsty over my parents every few minutes."

"If anyone has a right to be angsty, you do. And anyway, you're not being angsty. You're being real, and there's nothing wrong with that. Real doesn't scare me."

"Oh, yeah?"

"Real in someone else's life, I should say. Real in my own life still scares the crap out of me."

He smiled and took my hand again. Our fingers intertwined like they'd been made to fit together. When Robbie breathed a slow sigh and lay back on the bed, I lay back with him, and we gazed at the ceiling for a while. It was dotted with glow-in-the-dark plastic stars, the same kind I'd had on my bedroom ceiling when I was little.

"You know," he said, "I used to dream about going to space."

I glanced at him. His eyes were fixed on the stars above us, and he seemed to be serious. "Yeah?"

"Yeah. I imagined leaving everybody behind and starting a new life up there with some friendly aliens. I figured aliens would be so weird already that they wouldn't mind my weirdness, so I'd finally be able to fit in. Because I *really* didn't fit in. Even before I figured out I was trans, I wasn't very good at being normal."

"When did you know?" I asked quietly. "That you were trans, I mean."

"I don't know if there was ever one exact moment. It was more like a lot of little things all building up. Like, I remember crying when I had to wear a dress. Or wanting to go stand with the boys when the teacher lined us up in grade school. Stuff like that. Eventually it was just too much evidence to ignore."

"I always used to want to play the guy parts when my sisters and I played pretend," I said. "And I loved *The Little Mermaid.* That's supposed to be a big trans thing."

"Really?"

"Yeah, I mean Ariel wants to be part of a world society tells her she can't be a part of. She changes her body, defies her dad, and ends up living in her new body with the guy her family and her society didn't want her to fall in love with. It's all very, very trans and queer."

Robbie rolled onto his side to he could face me, his head pillowed on his arm. "When did you know?"

I chewed my lower lip while I thought about it. "Like you said, it was a lot of little things. The first time I started thinking about it was when I saw this super hot, buff guy in a movie and realized I didn't want to date him, I wanted to *be* him. But I guess the moment everything really came together for me was at the beginning of this past summer. I'd been researching being trans, reading things online and watching lots of videos, but I still wasn't totally sure. And then one day Mom took us over to the Dover Street pool, and I saw all these guys wearing their trunks and their board shorts and laughing and having a great time, and I just felt this longing, you know? It felt like I was supposed to be one of them, and when I saw myself in the changing room mirror, it was like I was looking at somebody else. Or like it was a costume I was wearing, but it wasn't who I really was.

"I've always felt kind of weird about my body. After I started getting—" I gestured vaguely towards my chest. "—you know, I couldn't look at myself in the mirror anymore. When I was younger, I even tried pushing down on them, like that would make them go back in or something. They just never felt right to me."

"Do you want to get surgery?" Robbie asked.

My first impulse was a resounding, *Yes!* But the truth was more complicated.

"I do. But I'm scared, too. What if something goes wrong? Or what if it doesn't look right after? The idea of taking off part of my body, even if it's a part I don't like, is pretty terrifying."

"It is," Robbie agreed. "It scares me, too, but then I imagine what it would feel like to just slide on a shirt and have it fit the way it's supposed to. And to be able to run in gym class without something pressing down on my chest the whole time. No more binder sweat, no more itching, no more feeling like I'm being suffocated. And to go swimming without a shirt on? *God*, I'd love that."

We both stared longingly into the distance, and I had to admit that when he put it like that, it was absolutely something I wanted.

"I've never been able to talk to anybody about stuff like this before," I said. "Thanks. It helps to know…"

"What?"

"That I'm not alone."

We spent a little more time trading trans boy stories on Robbie's bed, and then I noticed a cardboard box sitting on the nightstand. Robbie's deadname had been written on it in red magic marker and then scribbled out, replaced with "ROBBIE" in Maya's large, looping handwriting.

"Is that the stuff Maya gave you?" I asked.

Robbie grinned and got to his feet. He settled the box carefully between us on the bed and undid the cardboard flaps, and I leaned forward to peer inside.

There were piles of sketchbooks, notebooks, and loose sheets of paper, along with random photos and knick-knacks that had probably lived in Robbie's room before it was converted to storage. I saw a blue ribbon with "SPELLING" etched on it in gold lettering, a little glass jar of seashells, and what appeared to be a palm-sized rock on which someone had painted "Guitar Night" along with a stylized picture of a guitar puzzlingly surrounded by books. This was Robbie's life in a box, and my chest ached at the thought of it all packed away like this, gathering dust in Maya's room for the last six months instead of with Robbie where it belonged.

Robbie smiled as he rifled through the contents, occasionally lifting something of note to show me. "I made this in art class in second grade." He held up a lopsided ceramic mug with his initials scratched on the bottom. "I tried to bring Dad his coffee in it, but turns out second graders aren't great at ceramics, because it leaked all over the floor and made a huge mess. This—" He hefted the rock I'd already noticed. "—is from the first time I played guitar in public, at this open mic guitar night at the library. I was so nervous I almost broke one of my strings, but it turned out okay in the end." His eyes lit up as he pulled out a small, worn blue book with a gold tree emblazoned on the front. "And this was my first diary."

"Ooh." I leaned closer. "Are we about to find out all the scandalous secret thoughts of Young Robbie?"

Robbie scooted to sit with his back to the headboard of the bed, and I settled in next to him, our shoulders pressing warmly together as he opened the diary in his lap.

The handwriting within was messy and unpracticed, not quite managing to stay within the neat rows of lines. "June 1st," Robbie read. "Today I made a new friend. His name is Ty. I want to be like Ty. He is very smart and funny and can run very fast. I try to run fast, too, but I am too slow. Ty is a very cool guy. He is eight and I am only seven. I want to be a cool guy like Ty." Robbie cast me an amused glance. "Not exactly fine literature."

"I think it's great." I snuggled up against him and leaned my head on his shoulder as he flipped through the pages.

"August 8th. Today Maya and me played a new game with Ty. We went into Ty's treehouse and pretended we were a family living in the woods in the old times. But Maya and me got into a fight. I said I wanted to be Ty's husband but Maya said I couldn't be. She said if I wanted to marry Ty, I had to be a wife. I told her no and we fought about it until Ty said he didn't want a wife or a husband anyway. He wanted a dog."

Robbie and I both laughed.

"Ty's got his priorities straight," I said.

"Absolutely."

We browsed through some more entries, then found ourselves at the last entry in the book.

"October 27th." Robbie's voice softened as he read. "I am very sad and mad. I want to be a cowboy for Halloween, but Mama and Daddy say I have to be a cowgirl. I don't want to be a cowgirl. The pink hat is stupid and the outfit looks dumb. I want to be a cool tough cowboy like Ty. Ty gets to be a cowboy so I don't know why I can't be one too. Mama says I should stop hanging out with Ty because he is making me want to be a boy, but I told her that's not true. Ty is not making me do anything. She wouldn't listen and said I could be a cowgirl or not go trick-or-treating with Maya at all. I want to go trick-or-treating and get candy but I don't want to be a cowgirl so I don't know what to do. Maybe Ty can help. He always has good ideas."

There were no more entries in the diary after that, and Robbie flipped the book closed with a thoughtful expression on his face.

"What happened?" I asked softly. "With Halloween, I mean. Did you get to be a cowboy?"

Robbie gave a faint smile. "Kind of. I had to wear the cowgirl outfit, but Ty loaned me a cowboy hat and I wore that instead of the pink plastic one Mom wanted me to wear. Mom wasn't too happy, but at least it was kind of a compromise."

I wrapped my arm around his back, and he leaned into me and breathed out a slow, contented sigh.

"It's weird, looking back at this stuff. Even back then,

I always kind of knew who I was. I just didn't have the words to explain it yet."

"I wish I had stuff like this," I said. When Robbie arched a questioning eyebrow at me, I continued, "I mean, you can look back at this and say, 'Look, here, I always kind of knew I was trans.' But I don't have anything like that. No, I don't know…no proof, I guess."

Robbie quirked an eyebrow. "Leo, you don't need 'proof' to be trans."

"I know. But still, it'd be nice to have something like that."

Robbie turned to face me and took my hands in his. "Just because you didn't write it down doesn't mean you weren't feeling it. And even if you weren't feeling it then, so what? You feel it now, and that's just as real and valid as somebody who knew they were trans all along."

The reassurance warmed me, as it always did, and I told myself that sometime very soon, I would stop doubting myself and just be who I knew myself to be. Until then, though, it was good to know Robbie was around to remind me when I forgot.

After Robbie packed the box away again, he settled back down on the bed and faced me. He didn't say anything, just sat there with his eyes slowly tracing my face, and finally I gave a nervous laugh and flicked my gaze away from his.

"What?"

A faint flush colored his cheeks. "Sorry. I guess I just like looking at you."

I felt the same way about him, but the words still knocked the wind out of me. It was hard to believe anyone would like looking at *me*, but the sincerity was crystal clear in Robbie's voice.

"I, um. I like looking at you, too," I said.

He caught my arm and pulled, and we ended up lying side by side on the bed, facing each other with our heads resting on the same pillow. Robbie's fingers stroked up and down my arm, and I had a flash of vertigo at the realization that I was really here, lying in Robbie's bed feeling content and loved when a week ago I hadn't even known he existed.

"So," he murmured after we'd been drowsing in each other's warmth for a while. "Are you ever going to let me read one of your stories?"

I choked out an embarrassed laugh and pressed a hand to my face. "Agh, I don't know. They're really not very good. Though I did—" I snapped my mouth shut.

Robbie's lips pursed in question, his eyebrow lifting. "You did what?"

I considered changing the subject or finding some other way to wriggle out of answering, but in the end, I sighed and muttered, "I did start writing one that may or may not have a character who is maybe sort of a bit…like you."

Robbie propped his head up on his hand and beamed at me. "Seriously? You wrote me into a story?"

"I said *maybe*. But yes, hypothetically, I may have done that. And I may also have written myself into the same story, because I'm *that* guy."

"What kind of story is it?"

"Fantasy. I know it's not exactly considered 'high literature'—whatever that even means—but I love all that stuff. Elves, dwarves, mages, dragons… I should probably write more commercial fiction if I ever want to get published, but fantasy is just so *fun*."

Robbie looked far too delighted at this information. "So, what am I?"

"What do you mean?"

"Am I an elf, a mage, a dragon? I know I'm short, but don't say dwarf." When I hesitated, he laughed and shook my shoulder back and forth a few times. "Come on, you have to tell me at least that much."

I buried my face in the pillow. "Fine. You're a half-elf, and I'm a human mage, and we end up on a quest together and fall in love. And now I'm very embarrassed, so maybe we could talk about something else for a while."

I expected more laughter from Robbie, but when I peeled my face off the pillow, his expression was all warmth and tenderness.

"Hey," he said softly. "You really don't have to let me read it if you don't want to. I get it. I feel weird about showing people my drawings sometimes." He leaned closer, his thumb stroking my cheek. "But seriously? That sounds like an amazing story, and I love that you wrote me into it. And that I apparently like you just as much in the story as I do in real life."

He pressed his lips lightly to mine, and I smiled into it.

"Actually, we have sort of an enemies-to-lovers thing going on in the story, because I think that's more interesting—"

Robbie attempted to silence me with another kiss, and I happily let him.

We kissed for a bit longer, warm and soft and slow, and

then we ended up sitting on the floor with our arms around each other, watching random videos on Robbie's worn-out little laptop. His aunt found us like that an hour or so later, and her smile was just as bright as it had been every other time I'd seen her.

"Leo, I'm so glad you could come by!" Her dark bobbed hair bounced as she leaned over to plant a kiss on Robbie's cheek with a loud "Mwah!" "Robbie's really excited about coming to your birthday tomorrow. Oh, and guess what I found?"

Robbie was carefully avoiding my eyes, looking embarrassed but not unhappy at Allie's attention, but at this he brightened. "What?"

From behind her back, Allie produced what looked to be a dark suit on a hanger wrapped in plastic. "Ta-da! Found it at the thrift store. You'll have to try it on, of course, but I'm pretty sure it'll fit. And if it doesn't, we'll just have to risk me using the sewing machine again. I'm pretty sure I can figure out how to work it without anything catching on fire this time."

Robbie leaped to his feet with effusive thanks, reaching for the suit, but Allie held up her hand to stop him.

"Ah, ah, ah. Wait until Leo leaves before you try it on."

Robbie glanced back at me and frowned. "Why?"

"Because it's bad luck! He shouldn't see you in your suit until the big day."

"Allie, we're not getting married, I'm just going to his birthday party."

But Allie would not be persuaded, and she left us with a cheerful wave and the suit slung over her arm.

Robbie flopped onto the floor next to me and shook his head. “Sometimes I worry about her.”

But there was a warm smile on his face as he said it, and I could see how much it meant to him to have someone like Allie in his life. I leaned closer so I could wrap my arm around his waist and lean my head on his shoulder. He returned the favor, his arm going warmly around me, and we spent the rest of the afternoon drowsing together and watching videos. I couldn’t imagine a better way to spend my day.

Chapter Twenty-One

I hadn't seen Dad in my dreams for a few nights, but I'd been hoping he would show up the night before my birthday, if for no other reason than so I could tell him everything that had happened, how different and wonderful everything was now. But even when I envisioned the blue place with all the dream doors, he never showed, so I faced the doors on my own again and wondered what I should do.

I thought about visiting Robbie again, and the thought made me go warm all over. But, no, I didn't need to see him in my dreams. I saw him practically every day in reality, and that was so much better. I wondered vaguely what would happen if I pictured Dad, if I'd get a door that would lead me into whatever dreams he might be having from wherever he was now.

But when I closed my eyes, it was Jasmine's face that appeared in my mind. Jasmine, hurt and betrayed. Jasmine, sad and lost. Jasmine, who couldn't forgive me.

When I opened my eyes, the door in front of me was Jasmine's bedroom door, complete with a black sign edged in pink fluff that said, "Beware of the Princess" in gold letters. I knocked three times and waited.

Time passed and nothing happened. While I still couldn't quite believe any of this was real, the thought that Jasmine wouldn't want to let me in hurt. Would she really rather push me away than try to solve what had gone wrong between us?

Just as I was about to turn away, there was a soft click and the door crept open a millimeter. I hesitated, then pushed it the rest of the way open and stepped inside.

Robbie's dream had taken me to a grassy meadow and a family picnic. Jasmine's took me to a stormy sky and the rush of a violent ocean. Saltwater sprayed me in the face, and I blinked and sputtered until I spotted a figure sitting a little ways down the beach, perched on a big flat rock and staring out at the churning seawater.

My dream feet took me to the rock, and of course it was Jasmine who sat there, her knees drawn to her chest and her arms wrapped around them. She looked smaller, younger, and her hair was back to its natural brown. There was no makeup on her face, just olive skin and sadness and a few freckles. Her clothes, too, were plain and unadorned—a faded white T-shirt and blue jeans, a pair of worn sneakers she'd thrown out years earlier. No makeup, no jewelry, no hair dye. Just Jasmine.

"Jas?" I said softly.

She didn't turn. The ocean waves were reflected in her eyes.

"You know, I always wanted to be like you," she said.

Her voice was soft enough I should've had to strain to hear it over the crashing waves, but this was a dream, so I heard her loud and clear.

"All my life, you were this amazing older sister, this girl I thought I could never be. You were pretty, and funny, and cool, and you always listened to me when something was bugging me, even if it was stupid."

She gazed out at the ocean for another few beats, then shook her head.

"But then one day, things started to change. It was like… It was like you were hiding yourself from me. I'd look at you and I could just tell you were holding something back. I told you everything, all my secrets, but you didn't tell me what was really going on with you. You would rather push me away than let me in." She turned, finally, anguish brimming in her eyes. "Was it because you didn't trust me? Or because you thought I'd hate you?"

My voice was low, unsteady. "Don't you?"

"Of course I don't. But I don't understand how this happened. I don't know why I didn't already *know*. Why did you let me find out about this at school, from other people, instead of from you so I could understand and deal with it and be there for you?"

I sat down next to her on the rock. "Because I didn't know myself for a really long time. And after I figured it out, I was afraid. I didn't want to lose what we had either, and I knew that telling you who I was would change everything. Plus, you were always pushing me to dress like you, and anytime I dressed like myself, you gave me crap for it. I guess I was afraid you wouldn't be supportive, so I didn't tell you. I'm sorry. I know it was a mistake, but I was scared."

Tears glistened in her eyes. "I didn't… I'm sorry. I didn't know you felt like that. I just thought I was giving you fashion advice." Her gaze drifted back out to the ocean, and the waves gave a particularly violent crash against the rocks at our feet. "And I'm scared, too. I don't want to lose you."

"You haven't." And even though it was a dream and none of it mattered, I grabbed her hand and held it tightly in mine. "You never will. I keep telling you, I'm still me. The only thing that's different is the words. I'm not your sister, I'm your brother. Not she, he. That's the only thing that's changed. Just the words. That's all."

A faint, hopeful smile formed on her face, and in the distance, two blue-black storm clouds parted enough for a glimmer of sunlight to slip through.

Jeez, brain, going a little heavy on the metaphor, aren't we?

"Do you think things can ever be the same with us?" Jasmine asked.

I gripped her hand. "I don't think they'll be the same. I think they'll be better."

The dream faded away, and I woke up tangled in blankets and staring at the pale morning sunlight sneaking through the blinds to paint lines on my ceiling. The smile was still on my lips, but it faded with a sigh. My beautiful dream reconciliation with Jasmine might be helpful in figuring out what to say to the real Jasmine, but it didn't change the fact that we still had a lot of work to do before our relationship could be repaired.

I thought about trying to go back to sleep—it was barely after six, a glance at my alarm clock informed me—but then I remembered with a jolt that it was my birthday. A gorgeous blue suit was waiting for me in my closet, my best friends would be coming over later to celebrate with me and my family, and every person who would be in attendance at the party knew I was a guy. Suddenly the thought of wasting the day lying in bed just didn't seem appealing anymore.

I crawled out of bed with a yawn and a stretch, and I was halfway through opening the window blinds when my door burst open. Before I could turn, someone threw their arms around my midsection and clung to me from behind.

I gave a surprised "oof!" and tried to spin around to see who'd tackled me.

"I'm so sorry." Jasmine's voice was muffled as she buried her face in the back of my nightshirt. "I'm so sorry I acted like this. You're right. It's just words, right? It's just the words that are different, but you're still you and it's all going to be okay."

I staggered back and struggled to find my voice. "I—*What?*"

Jasmine clung to me for another few seconds, then let go and stepped back, wiping her eyes. "Look, I know it doesn't make any sense, but I had to tell you. I'm sorry, and I'm going to try to do better, I promise. I love you. I love you, Leo!"

She fled the room before I could answer, and I sank into my desk chair feeling winded. As I stared mutely around the room, trying to make the last thirty seconds of my life make sense, my gaze caught on the framed picture on my shelf, the only framed picture in my room. It was a photo of Dad in his late teens. He was wearing a puffy brown jacket and posing next to a motorcycle, his curly hair wild and windswept. His crooked grin seemed to be laughing at a joke he hadn't shared with anyone else.

He laughed at me from behind the glass of the frame, and I laughed, too, and cried a little, because if the dream with Jasmine had been real, then everything else had been real, too.

"Dad," I whispered. I wiped the moisture from my cheeks and closed my eyes. "Thank you."

Chapter Twenty-Two

I met Robbie at the door. Behind me, Mom bustled around in the kitchen getting hors d'oeuvres onto the appropriate trays, and somewhere in the distance Maribel and Eleanor were squealing with laughter and saying, "Uncle Shel, no!" But all I could focus on was Robbie.

"Hey," I said. I felt a little breathless.

"Hey," he said. He sounded a little breathless, too.

He stood on our front porch in a black suit with a deep purple tie. There was a fray or two on the collar, but otherwise the suit looked brand new despite its thrift store origins, and it fit him beautifully.

Instead of letting him in, I stepped outside to join him and closed the front door behind me. The sunny afternoon had settled into a cool blue evening, and everything was dim and quiet and peaceful. The trees and houses across the road made dark outlines against the sky.

"Thanks for coming," I said. "I know it might be weird, coming to a family party when we haven't even really known each other for that long, but—"

"No, I'm glad you asked me." He glanced down at

himself self-consciously. "Do I, um. Am I dressed okay? I know it's not exactly the finest formalwear, but..."

I laughed. "Are you kidding? You look fantastic."

Some of his self-consciousness melted away under a shy smile. "Thanks. And you—" His voice went low and fervent. "You look amazing."

The devotion in his voice tingled through me, and I wrapped my arms around him and kissed him. We might've done that for quite some time had a horn not honked in the driveway and Jackson shouted, "Hey, get a room!"

"Hi, Jackson!" Robbie called cheerfully. Although he looked regretful our kiss had been interrupted, he opted for taking my hand and swinging it between us as Jackson swaggered up the walk.

Jackson had defaulted to the gray suit he wore to church services with his parents, though he'd jazzed it up by tucking a bright blue flower into the lapel—plastic, if I was any judge, but the effort was there.

"Lookin' good, my dudes," he said with an approving glance at our respective suits. "Leo, I never thought of you in blue, but I like it. Very dapper, my man."

"Thanks," I said. "Mr. Raines picked it out."

"Mr. Raines? Our Mr. Raines? Teacher Mr. Raines?"

"He's here, by the way. Mom invited him and his husband."

"Him and his—" There was a long pause as Jackson studied me. "I'm getting the feeling I've missed a few things."

I grinned and wrapped my arm around his neck as best I could without letting go of Robbie's hand. "I'll fill you in later, I promise."

Jackson extricated himself from my arm so he could reach for the front door knob, but the rev of an engine made us all pause.

Robbie's hand went tense in mine as a fancy black car stopped at the edge of our driveway—not too close, not actually in the driveway—so Maya could get out of the passenger seat. The dimness of the evening made it hard to see, but I could just make out the outline of Robbie's dad through the windshield. I hadn't been planning to say anything, but the stiffness of Robbie's shoulders and the sadness in his eyes were the last straw. I stepped forward to the edge of the porch and shouted.

"Hey! You know this guy is amazing, right? You know you're lucky to have him as your son? He's smart and funny and kind and wonderful, and if you can't see that, then that's your loss! You're the one who suffers here, because you don't get to have this awesome person in your life!"

There was a moment of stunned silence, and then Jackson jabbed his finger at the black car and yelled, "Yeah!"

Maya went back to the car to say something to her dad through the window, and then she turned her back on him and started up the walk. I finally dared to look at Robbie, hoping I hadn't hopelessly embarrassed him, but he was gazing back at me with a startled smile on his face.

"You didn't have to say that," he said.

"I know. But I needed to. Somebody had to say it."

Maya reached the porch just as the car made a three-point turn and sped off the way it had come. She watched it go a little sadly, then ducked in to hug Robbie, then me. A subtle flowery scent clung to her, and her hair was a beautiful dark halo around her. I wasn't sure what I'd been expecting her to wear, but I loved what she'd settled on, a deep blue saree with intricate gold and silver flowers embroidered along the sleeves and neckline.

"What did you say to him?" Robbie asked.

Maya met his eyes. "I said, 'he's right,' because he is. You *are* awesome."

We made our way indoors, Robbie's hand still in mine and Jackson griping to Maya about how everyone had gotten a hug but him. Mom waited just inside the door in her best dark-blue dress. Her eyes went from my face to Robbie's and down to our joined hands, and then she swept forward and gathered Robbie to her in a tight Momly hug.

"You listen to me," she said, while Robbie held his arms out like a starfish and gave me a panicked look over Mom's shoulder. "You are welcome here. You are welcome here *always*, and I think it's just wonderful that you and my— that you and my son are so close."

She pulled back, brushed some tears from her eyes, and smiled at us. "Well, go enjoy the party. I have a few things to finish up in the kitchen, and then I'll be out to join you."

Robbie still looked a little unsteady, so I put my arm around him and led him and the others through the house to the backyard. Since the weather had been kind enough to cooperate, Mom, Uncle Shel, and I had rigged up some string lights and set up buffet tables, chairs, and even a little Bluetooth speaker for the enjoyment of the party-goers.

When we got out there, the party was in full swing. Mr. Raines and his husband were dancing to *December 1963 (Oh, What A Night)*—and singing along in impressively off-key voices—while Grandma Pearl and Grandpa Earl sat nearby in wooden folding chairs with heaping plates of food balanced on their laps. Grandma was wiping a bit of potato salad off Grandpa's chin with a napkin, and Grandpa was bopping along to the music like he might get up and dance at any second.

Aunt Audrey, I was surprised to see, was playing a game with Maribel and Eleanor that involved chasing each other in a circle and then falling down on the grass, and while Audrey was doing the falling down part pretty half-heartedly, only sort of kneeling and tilting her head down while the twins flopped down below her, the smile on her face was the most genuine one I'd seen since she'd been here. Uncle Shel stood a few feet away, pretending to fiddle with the lights while stealing glances at his wife with a warm smile on his lips.

Eliza was at the buffet table in her best white dress with a skinny red-haired girl, and somehow they were managing to spoon vegan mac and cheese onto their plates while also holding hands and occasionally looking at each other, blushing, and smiling.

"Jeez, is everybody at this thing paired off except me?" Jackson said with a woeful look at Eliza and Becky.

"Not everybody," Maya reminded him with a lift of her eyebrow.

"Oh. Right. Sorry."

"I don't suppose you'd want to dance?" Maya asked.

Jackson threw her an awkward look. "Uh, I'd love to, but just so you know, I'm gay."

Maya grinned and held out her hand. "So am I. So what?"

Later, she would confess to me that on the first day of school, while Aspen had come up to me hoping I was a guy, Maya had come up to me hoping I wasn't. They'd both ended up disappointed.

"Oh, my God." Joy trembled through me until I wanted to laugh out loud. "There are *so many queer people* at my house right now."

Maya and Jackson had already gone to join Mr. Raines and his husband by the speaker, so Robbie was the only one close enough to hear me. He laughed and took my hand, and soon we were dancing with the others. When a slow song came on the playlist, I had the great pleasure of wrapping my arms around the boy I liked and swaying back and forth with him to the music. Mr. Raines and Leo had headed over to the buffet by this point, and I heard Grandma Pearl saying loudly to them, "I think it's nice that you're both so tall. Earl and I always had trouble dancing together because I'm so much shorter than he is, but you two never have that problem, do you?"

I laughed into Robbie's shoulder and held him closer.

The song had just ended when the back door opened and Jasmine stepped out. She wore the blue sequined dress Mom had bought for me, and it fit her perfectly. Her hair was down, and I was surprised to see she'd dyed it back to brown.

The sight of it snapped me back to the day I'd come home with my hair cut: Mom had been surprised but supportive, gushing about what a great haircut it was for summer, and Eliza, Maribel, and Eleanor had glanced at my shorn locks and then gone back to what they were doing (Eliza reading, Maribel and Eleanor building a wobbling tower of stuffed animals on the living room couch).

But Jasmine had gone absolutely silent, her face blank and unreadable. And while she normally would've been the first to offer her thoughts on anything related to hair, makeup, or fashion, this time she didn't say a word.

That night, I walked in on her bleaching her hair in the bathroom. When I asked what she was doing, she shrugged and avoided my eyes in the mirror. "I've wanted to try dying it for a while, but since we had the whole twinning thing going, I didn't want to mess that up. But now that that's done, I figured I might as well." Her expression and posture were casual and uncaring, but her words were oddly clipped. Before I could reply, she turned her back on me. "Close the door on your way out."

At the time, I'd just figured she was in one of her occasional bad moods. But that hadn't been it at all, had it? I hadn't only distanced myself from Jasmine, I'd changed everything about myself that connected us. For all our closeness, we'd never had a ton of shared interests. I was into anime, classic rock, and anything action or fantasy, and Jasmine loved rom-coms, Taylor Swift, and creepy shows about serial killers. The only thing we'd had in common was looking alike, and I'd ripped that away from her without a word of explanation. Of *course* she was hurt. Of course she did whatever small thing she could to show she didn't want to be associated with me, either.

I breathed out a long, slow breath that released months of tension from my body.

But we could finally put all that behind us, couldn't we?

Jasmine stopped in front of Robbie and offered him a small smile. "Do you mind if I dance with my brother?"

Robbie stepped back, warmth shining from his eyes. "Go ahead." He brought my hand to his lips and kissed it before leaving us, and I faced Jasmine with what was probably a very silly grin on my face.

She shook her head and put her hands on my shoulders. I rested my hands on her waist, and we swayed.

"You look nice," she said.

"You, too," I said. "Is that…?"

"I hope you don't mind. Mom was going to take it back, but I asked her if I could have it. All we had to do was raise the hem a little, and it fit perfectly." Her eyes locked onto mine for an instant before shifting back to the world beyond my shoulder. "It's important to have clothes that fit you, isn't it?"

"It is." The blue suit felt particularly nice against my skin, and since I'd put it on I'd been standing taller than usual, feeling stronger and more confident. More like myself. "How are you feeling? About everything?"

"I'm okay," she said. "I'm still having some trouble with all this, but I'm getting there, you know? I thought I knew who you were, and when I realized I didn't, it really threw me. But just because you're not who I thought you were doesn't mean you're not still the same person. It's like if I look at some stranger and think it's Chris Hemsworth and it turns out it isn't. It's not his fault he's not Chris

Hemsworth. It's my fault for making the mistake in the first place."

I swallowed a laugh. "Are you trying to tell me I look like Chris Hemsworth?"

She rolled her eyes. "You wish. But you do, um. You do make a good-looking guy, just so you know. Most of the people at school asking me if I had a brother were girls, and they were asking because they thought you were hot. So. That's a thing." Her gaze flickered to the buffet table, where Robbie was talking with Mr. Raines and Leo while they scooped taco salad onto their plates. "Though I'm guessing you don't want me to get you any of their numbers, huh?"

"No thanks," I said. "I mean, not that I'm not flattered and—really surprised, to be honest. But yeah, I think I've found what I'm looking for."

The song ended, and Jasmine took a step back and looked up at me. "It's not going to be weird between us anymore, is it? Because if I can't have my big sister, I'd really kind of like to have my big brother."

"You will." I took her hand and gave it a good squeeze. "You do."

She squeezed back, then turned and walked away. Robbie, Jackson, and Maya found me soon afterward, and we alternated our time between dancing like idiots to random oldies, stuffing ourselves with food from the buffet, and chatting with Mr. Raines and Leo, Grandma and Grandpa, Mom, my sisters, Uncle Shel, and even Aunt Audrey.

Finally, when pretty much everyone had had their fill

of the buffet, Mom clanged a fork against her glass. "Well, I think it's time for cake and presents now, don't you?"

A general cheer of approval went up—and an excited squeal from Maribel and Eleanor—and a minute later Mom emerged from the back door carrying a big rectangle of a white sheet cake with sixteen candles blazing on top of it.

I'd never liked this part of my birthday, as everyone's eyes were on me and I had to stand still and smile awkwardly while people sang to me, but this year I just relaxed and enjoyed it. Especially when every voice in the yard sang, "Happy birthday, dear *Leo*." My heart felt ridiculously full, and I was grinning as I leaned over to blow out the candles.

Once I'd done so, I finally noticed the details of the cake, and I grinned at the blue frosted bow and the words, "IT'S A BOY!" traced in blue icing across the top.

Presents were next, which I opened while Mom cut slices of cake at the table beside me. There was a card with fifty dollars in it from Grandma and Grandpa—very much appreciated—a card and a mall gift certificate from Aunt Audrey and Uncle Shel—also great—and a hardcover book called *Cemetery Boys* from Mr. Raines and Leo, with a little sticky note in Mr. Raines' loopy handwriting that said, "Pretty sure you'll like this."

I'd told my friends they didn't need to bring any gifts, but Maya still stepped forward with a little white box that turned out to contain a rainbow flag pin, and Jackson handed me a bag of vegan peanut butter cups, which he had ordered online after I'd whined to him a while back about how unfair it was that regular peanut butter cups had milk in them.

“Now maybe you’ll finally shut up about it,” he said with a grin.

“I promise I will,” I said. “Seriously, thank you. These are all going to be gone by morning, though, I hope you know.”

He handed me a piece of paper. “Here’s where you can order more. I’d get them for you, but I don’t have that kind of cash to burn, you know?”

I figured that was the end of the presents, but Robbie approached me shyly and pulled a square of notebook paper out of his pocket. “It’s really not much,” he said, “but I hope you like it.”

I unfolded it and found a pencil sketch of my face. It was beautifully done, the lines dark and confident, and somehow Robbie hadn’t just captured the look of me but the essence, too. There was something very *me* about every line and curve of the sketch, a combination of hope and strength in the tilt of my eyebrows and the slight upward turn of my lips.

“I started it on the first day of school.” Robbie ducked his head as Jackson and Maya both craned around to see the drawing. “In Geometry. Mr. Raines caught me doing it, but he let me keep working on it.”

“You old romantic, you,” Leo said from where he stood with his arm intertwined with Mr. Raines’.

“It’s perfect,” I told Robbie. “Thank you. Honestly, I love it.” As he beamed at me, I turned to the assembled guests. “Well, I guess that’s—”

"One more!" Mom jogged out through the back door with a small wrapped parcel cradled to her chest. "There's one more present."

She dropped the gift into my hands, and my fingers closed over something hard and oddly shaped wrapped in a thick piece of white cloth.

"Sorry for the wrapping job," Mom said. "I actually had a gold necklace I was going to give you, but I took it back and figured this would be a better fit. I thought about getting you something else from the store, but this just seemed more meaningful."

I unwrapped the cloth and the breath caught in my throat.

"Dad's watch," I breathed.

"I think he would've wanted you to have it," Mom said. "And more than that, I want you to have it."

The watch was heavy, the gold cool against my skin. It took a few tries and some help from Jackson to get it fastened, but finally it was there on my wrist, Dad's watch and now my watch. The string lights glittered on the dark face of it like stars, and the reflection of my own face shimmered there among them, smiling and grateful.

"Thank you," I said, and I meant the words for my mom, my family, my friends, Dad, the world, the universe, everything. Anyone and anything that had brought me to this moment.

The party went on for another hour or so, and then the guests headed home, family members retired to bedrooms, and it was just Mom and me cleaning up in the backyard. We did so in silence for a while, but eventually I had to ask.

"Are you sure about me having this?" I lifted my wrist so Dad's watch flashed in the porch light. "I know how much it means to you."

"It does mean a lot to me. But so do you." Her gaze flitted past the unfinished treehouse, which I'd already quietly asked Shel if he could help me fix up before he left, and then she turned back to the food she was scooping out of the aluminum trays and into glass containers. "You know, it might sound silly, but I dream about him sometimes. Your dad."

I perked up but tried not to sound too eager. "You do?"

"Yeah. Sometimes they're just regular dreams, but other times they feel so real. It's like he's really there, visiting me. I had one just the other night, actually. He was wearing that watch, and that's what gave me the idea to give it to you."

While I was still reeling, she smiled and patted my shoulders. "Why don't you go get ready for bed? I'll finish up here. It doesn't seem right, you having to clean up after your own birthday party."

I surveyed the utter havoc we'd visited on the backyard. "Mom, this is a *lot* for one person to clean up."

"Oh, don't worry." Mom's smile was faintly evil. "I have a feeling Audrey is just dying to help me."

I laughed and went inside, and a little while later I looked out my window and saw Audrey and Mom tidying up the backyard. Their voices rose to me every now and then, and it sounded like they were laughing.

Before I went to sleep that night, I settled Dad's framed photo on my nightstand and sat Robbie's drawing next to it so I could look at both of them as I fell asleep. I drifted off almost immediately, warm and content and wishing every day could end like this one.

Chapter Twenty-Three

As I stood in my dreamscape, I realized there was nothing I could dream that could top the night I'd just had. I'd brought my blue suit into the dream with me, and Dad's watch was a comforting weight on my wrist, fitting a little more snugly in the dream than it had in real life. Mom had said it would be easy enough to take it to the jeweler's and get it sized down, but I didn't mind if it was a little loose. And who knew? Maybe I'd grow into it.

"It looks good on you," came a voice from behind me, and I spun around with my heart in my throat.

Dad was there. He wasn't in the Steelers' sweatshirt or his yellow polo shirt, but wearing the dark blue suit we'd buried him in. But while the face in the coffin had been slack and lifeless, the one I looked at now was warm and open and full of love.

He looked me up and down, the son he'd never known he had, and I tried to stand tall and confident and strong when all I wanted to do was run to him and hug him. His face broke into a crooked smile, the same one from the framed photo I'd fallen asleep looking at.

"Did it help you?" he asked. "The dreaming."

"It did." And then, because I had to ask: "Why me, Dad? Why did you teach me how to do this and not Jasmine or Eliza or one of the twins?"

Dad gave me a soft smile. "Not everyone in our family has the ability. I've visited your sisters, and I'm so glad I had the chance to spend time with them, but they never saw me for what I was. They just saw a dream. But you saw *me*, and that's how I knew I'd be able to teach you. And you've done so well. I'm so proud of you."

I swallowed. "This is the last time, isn't it? The last time you'll be here."

He nodded sadly. "I'm glad I got to see you. The real you." He drew forward and rested his hand on my shoulder. His smile was soft, his eyes dark and kind. "You're a good boy, and you're going to grow up to be an amazing man. Just don't make the same mistake I did, okay?"

"What mistake did you make?"

He gave a sad smile. "Not appreciating it enough when I had it."

I did hug him, then, and he was solid and real and when his arms tightened around me, I remembered every bad dream he'd comforted me over, every late-night cough he'd cured with a hot cup of tea and honey, every time he'd come home and swept me up into his arms and swung me around in a circle. He'd been a good man and a very good father, and I could only pray I'd turn out to be half as good when my turn came.

"I love you, Dad," I whispered.

"I love you, too," Dad said. "Son."

• • •

Life didn't magically become perfect and easy after my sixteenth birthday. There were still problems and school bullies and the usual supply of angst, and my family and I still got into arguments. Even Jackson, Maya, Robbie, and I had our disagreements and tense moments, but it was all okay because I got to be me through it all. I got to be Leo Torres, sixteen-year-old guy, brother, son, friend, boyfriend, and baritone. I got to make mistakes and do stupid things as myself, and that made all the difference.

The Colorado relatives ended up staying with us for an extra week, and that gave Uncle Shel and me enough time to fix up the treehouse Dad had never finished building. Maribel and Eleanor clambered up into it gleefully the minute it was done, and I stood proudly next to Shel admiring our handiwork. When Mom came home that night and saw what we'd done, she cried and hugged us and said Dad would've been so proud. I was pretty sure she was right.

When Grandma, Grandpa, Shel, and Audrey piled into Mom's car to head back to the airport, Shel left me with a worn but sturdy toolbelt, a hammer and nails, a screwdriver, and a variety of other tools he'd dug out of the big red toolbox he'd brought with him from Colorado. A week later, a package came for me in the mail that turned out to be a sturdy black toolbox of my own and a power drill, plus a dog-eared book on home repair with Uncle Shel's untidy writing all through the margins. I grinned as I flipped through it and thought about the wobbly end table in the living room. I figured I might even have a go at the three-wheeled skateboard, provided Mom hadn't found it in my closet and burned it to ashes by now.

Not long after that, we got word that Aunt Audrey and Uncle Shel had decided to become foster parents, and at Christmas time, we got a card with Audrey, Shel, and two twin boys who couldn't have been more than five years old grinning at us with Santa hats on their heads and a glittering Christmas tree behind them. Audrey looked happier than I'd ever seen her, and Shel had one big hand on each of the boys' shoulders, looking every inch the proud foster father. Mom hung the card in a place of honor in the center of the mantlepiece, and every time I looked at it, I felt warm inside.

I didn't use the dream doors much after Dad's last visit. It felt like they'd done their job, and I didn't want to intrude on my friends' and family's dreams when I had so many of my own to build. But every now and then, I'd slip in through Robbie's door and stand with him against whatever nightmares his past sent his way, and it seemed to help. I never told him about it, but he always looked at me a little more tenderly the morning after, like everything he'd ever wanted was right there in my face and the warm press of my hand. I felt the same way about him.

Robbie and his aunt Allie spent Christmas Eve with us, and Maya biked over to join us for dinner. Robbie's parents still hadn't come around, but they had finally signed the paperwork to make Allie Robbie's official legal guardian, which made a lot of things simpler. I couldn't imagine how much it hurt Robbie to be cast off by his parents, but he was definitely better off living with someone like Allie who adored him and supported him.

And my family was more than happy to unofficially adopt him—he spent so much time at our place that Allie had started complaining that she hardly saw him anymore, and Maribel and Eleanor were apparently going around school telling everyone they had two brothers now instead of one. They'd been so adamant about it that Mom had received a "Congratulations On Your New Baby" card signed by the entire class of fourth graders, and that, too, had received a place of honor on the mantle.

After Christmas Eve dinner, everyone retired to the living room to play games, but Robbie and I slipped into the family room and curled up together on the couch by the fireplace. I lay in back, my arms around Robbie's waist, and tucked my chin in the crook of his shoulder as we watched the flames peacefully flickering.

"You know," Robbie said, "I'm really glad my charter school closed down."

I laughed. I also couldn't help noticing that after a month on testosterone, Robbie's voice had already dipped into a slightly lower register. I couldn't wait until I could start, too, though Mom was having me wait at least another few months "just to be on the safe side." The safe side of what, I wasn't really sure, but she'd always been the cautious type.

"Me, too." I snuggled closer.

"So," he murmured. "Got any new chapters for me to read? Because, honestly—and I'm not just saying this to earn boyfriend points—that would be a pretty great Christmas present."

I chewed on my lower lip as I fought a smile. "I may or

may not have finished the last chapter the day before yesterday."

He jerked his neck around as best he could to stare at me. "Seriously? You finished it? The whole story?"

I wrapped my arms more snugly around his waist and rested my chin on his shoulder. "Yep. I may also have printed it all out and had it professionally bound with that sketch you did of our characters on the front cover, because as you already know, I'm a massive dork."

He grinned and planted a quick kiss on my cheek. "I wouldn't have it any other way. So, what happens to Rael the half-elf and Simon the human mage? Do they make it out okay?"

"Nope, no spoilers from me. You'll just have to read it and find out."

He groaned, and I turned him in my arms so we were face to face, so I could stare directly into his warm brown eyes and stroke his cheek. God, I loved him. It was kind of ridiculous how much.

"Just between you and me?" I said softly. "I'm pretty sure they live happily ever after."

As we settled back in to watch the fire together, I remembered being on the phone with Robbie months earlier and him asking me to imagine my future. Back then, all I'd been able to imagine was that I'd be living as a guy, no other details. But now, when I thought about what was ahead, I saw myself with a deeper voice and a chin covered in stubble, a flat chest with scars but no binder. I saw a writer spinning epic fantasy stories that may or may not be any good, but were at least something that made him—and his boyfriend—very happy.

I saw myself with the toolbox Shel had given me, going through life fixing what was broken, leaving things better than when I'd found them. I saw myself posing for a Christmas card with an indeterminate amount of kids crowding around me, calling me "Dad" and asking if they could play with the gold watch that always sat on my wrist. I saw Robbie there beside me, the two of us moving from trans boyhood into manhood together, and then… Who knew. Anything. Anything could happen.

Anything we could dream.

About the Author

T.J. Baer is a queer, trans author of both adult and young adult LGBTQ+ fiction. Born in Western Pennsylvania, he currently resides in his adopted hometown of Chicago with two cats and a well-stocked cupboard of tea. When not writing, T.J. can be found either discussing queer media on his YouTube channel or failing to escape from murderous ghosts on Twitch.

Also from Deep Hearts YA

A Broke Boy in a Rich Girl's Heart
C.K. Dion

Sallie lives a comfortable life in a wealthy resort town. Things seem to go well in her life, from her parents supporting her transition to her budding businesses making jewelry to her awesome best friend.

This comfortable life takes an unexpected detour—the good kind—when she meets fellow teen artist Cris. While the start of their friendship is awkward, he quickly becomes an important part of her life and those feelings soon grow. That chance meeting blossoms into a relationship with both teens head over heels in love.

But not everyone is happy about this.

The problem? Cris comes from the wrong part of town and Sallie's parents have a problem with that. They'd rather see her with someone like Aidan—good looks, athletic, respectable family, great wealth—than someone like Cris.

With endless obstacles and challenges thrown in their way, will this broke boy find a permanent place in this rich girl's heart?

Available now in ebook and paperback

Also from Deep Hearts YA

Stone Feather Fang
A.G. Rodriguez

The gods—the cemi—have left the world of Ke', and their lush and verdant Andolin Islands are now inhabited by impious followers.

Teenage priestess Hildy Rios is tasked with saving her religion. In a special ritual called the Telling, she must somehow reawaken her people's love of the gods. Her effort is the last hope of her people: after this Telling, there will be no more chances, as the cemi will vanish into the past, their power forever lost to the world of Ke'.

The weight of her world on her shoulders, Hildy rewrites the Telling's story—and her own. She weaves a tale of her distant ancestor, a boy named Jenaro, blessed with the ability to see and speak to the cemi; a boy who, though long past, becomes as much a part of the present by way of the Telling's power.

For three days, Hildy brings to life the tale of Jenaro and his yearning for adventure, how he is haunted by the cemi of death, and who—like her—is fighting against the shackles of his family and society. For three days, Jenaro becomes real, and the power of the cemi to reach across time should be enough to convince Ke's people, but their impiety runs so deep…

Hildy and Jenaro. Two people joined by cursed blood, but separated by centuries of time. Only the cemi know how their tales will end.

Available now in ebook and paperback

www.ingramcontent.com/pod-product-compliance
Lightning Source LLC
Chambersburg PA
CBHW030133010826
48973CB00002B/538
9781998055623